S{E}AN?

I0618055

Published simultaneously in the United States and
Great Britain in 2015 by Pretend Genius

Copyright © Sean Brijbasi

This book is copyright under the Berne Convention
No reproduction without permission
All rights reserved

ISBN: 978-0-9852133-6-7

other books by Sean Brijbasi

One Note Symphonies
for Emma

Still Life in Motion
for those who play
Marius and Andréus

The Unknowed Things
for Julius

The Dictionary of Coincidences, Volume i
for Emma

S{E}AN?

for
em{m}a+

Of all that is written, I love only what ~~a person~~ S{E}AN? has written with his own blood.

--Fri+edrich Wil!helm Nietzs/c/he

Part 1

S{E}AN? DISAPPEARS

i

Fever cried when she heard the news. The boy with the curly, black hair who made me laugh the time he fell on the ground to play dead had gone missing. His father said they last saw him the morning before as he walked to school. We thought we heard his grandfather in the background mumbling something about the Germans. His mother couldn't bring herself to speak. His uncle said his nephew liked to invent new words and pretend that he could only see out of one eye. I never caught the boy's name but I remember his face. *Maybe he ran away*, I thought. His parents didn't seem like the type to ruin a kid but you never know. Maybe he just couldn't take it anymore. Fever stood by the dresser and put on her watch. It was a gift from me for her birthday though I never had it engraved.

"I have to go", she said.

She's going to come over here before she leaves I thought, *she loves me.*

"Okay", I said.

She turned off the TV, walked over to the bed, and kissed me.

"I'll call you later", she said. "Get going."

I didn't care what Fever did anymore. *You get the fuck going.* It was all brandy and plums for her but I had already started to despise her. It was something that had built up in me without me realizing it until it was too late. A slur here and there. A sigh. An objection. And then one day I hated her. I had explored the feeling for a few days to understand what I was feeling. I wondered if it was a feeling that I could change or if the feeling would change on its own. But hating her no longer bothered me.

"Let me be clear," I said to myself. "I feel nothing for you."

If she despised me also it would be easy. What I didn't want was all the drama, the talking-about-it, the crying, the *hold me.* I could take a chance that she felt the same way and then there could be a clean break between us. But if she didn't feel the same way then I might have to console her and that would make me despise her even more.

The first night *I felt nothing for her* I stayed downstairs a little bit longer than I usually did and missed some of the show that we watched together. The next night I missed the entire show. I told her I was tired of it all—that I had grown weary of the same theme and the same characters. I hated how I felt while I was watching it. And one night I didn't go upstairs until after she fell asleep. Instead I walked from room to room—a choreography borne of disgust and exhaustion. We took this picture and that picture. She liked this lamp. I liked that chair. I thought about the trivial conversations we had and decided that my life had descended into a labyrinth of the trivial.

ii

When Fever and I first met we didn't talk like I thought people normally talked. We were clever. Or at least clever*ish*. I talked about philosophy and art. She talked about science and architecture. We'd hold hands across the table from each other.

"That's a good example of ship architecture", she would say.

"Spinoza might have taken issue with that", I would say.

And it was all sweet and sexy air until we got to know each other just a little bit more.

"Are you sure? I've read differently."

"You can think that if you want to but that's not what studies have shown."

And then it was only a matter of time before our hands separated—she to reach into her purse and me to fiddle with the menu one more time. I always waited for her to pull her hand away before I started to pull mine away so that it would seem like we pulled away at the same time.

But I didn't feel like getting out of bed that morning. Invent new words? I took a shower. Again. I took a shower the night before as a way of trying to communicate with Fever. I left the bathroom door open so she could hear the water. It was my way of trying to reach out to her.

Yesterday morning I ironed one of my shirts while she lay in bed (longer than I had ever ironed a shirt before). Each hiss of steam from the iron was a plea. But she didn't notice. Or maybe she did notice and just decided to ignore my pleas.

I needed to pee, although I practiced holding it for emergencies. When I passed the bedroom window I saw a flash of human in our small backyard. I looked out and saw a boy jumping over our fence into another yard. My armpits perspired. I waited and saw a ball go into the air. The brothers who lived behind us were playing catch.

I once knew a woman who had been married for thirty years and when her youngest son went to university, her husband left her for a twenty year old Brazilian girl. He even moved to Brazil to live with her. Just like that. After all that time together.

iii

I don't understand people who want to hurt children. But then I don't have children and I don't spend too much time around them. The boys who lived behind us seemed friendly enough. I wasn't sure how to talk to them but they wouldn't want to talk to me anyway.

I was bored but didn't want to turn on the TV because I didn't want to see any bad news. I didn't want to see any good news either. I wanted a neutral day (a day in which goodness and badness were affected by my own thoughts and actions and not by the thoughts and actions of someone else). But Deaf called me which usually tilted the day to one side or the other of neutral.

We called him Deaf because he was always saying "huh?" or "what'd you say?" even though he'd heard us. He said it was part of his mental preparation for whatever concise answer he was about to give us. He quoted Shakespeare and Nietzsche and had degrees in literature and economics. I guess that made him a genius. He wasn't smarter than my Dad but he was almost just as smart, which gave me hope because my Dad and I were genetically related.

Deaf and I had a bet one time about Henry V. He won, of course. I mentioned to Fever afterwards that I wanted to become a Shakespeare scholar. She laughed at me but I was only half-joking. As far as I was concerned quoting Shakespeare made you sound like a genius even if you weren't one. That's all I really wanted.

"What are you doing on Friday night?" he asked me.

“I don’t know”, I said. “I haven’t talked to Fever yet.”

“What? Let’s hang out”, he said.

“Okay”, I said. “I’ll tell Fever it’s your birthday. When is your birthday by the way?”

“Huh? Well, we’ll just say it’s on Friday so you won’t be compromised.”

I called Fever and told her I was going out with Deaf on Friday because it was his birthday. She said she wanted to go to the neighborhood watch meeting the neighborhood watchers were having that night and that she wanted me to go with her. She said she knew Deaf’s birthday was in December and that I was an idiot for thinking I had to lie.

“Why are we going to a neighborhood watch meeting?” I asked.

I ignored the idiot and lying part (it was the most human thing I’d done in weeks).

“To see if there’s anything we can do to help find that boy who disappeared”, she said. “I mean, it happened in our neighborhood, on our street.”

Neighborhood watch meeting? What the fuck were we gonna do? The kid’s photograph was all over the place and the police were looking for him. And who holds a neighborhood watch meeting on a

Friday night? I didn't even consider this place my neighborhood. We rented.

"Uhm, okay. Deaf and I are going to start early so maybe", I said.

Meaning maybe the fuck not.

iv

On Sunday evening Fever went out and I was left to finish the laundry and clean up. I kissed her good-bye and started on those damn clothes right away. I did love Fever despite my feelings for her. I *what-I-call* finished the laundry in about an hour. I wasn't staying at home while Fever was out having fun. I cleaned myself up, got dressed (in freshly laundered clothes), locked the door behind me, and started walking to the bus stop. I planned on catching the bus but a car pulled over and stopped for me. I got in and sat in the backseat with two girls. They asked me where I was going (nowhere). They said they were going to the Tractor Club (the Tractor Club!). I'd always wanted to go there (I imagined a neon cow on the roof) but it wasn't Fever's style.

"Yeah, I'm going there too", I said.

When we got to the club we sat shoulder to shoulder to shoulder.

"Wanna go outside for a smoke?" one of the girls asked me.

“Sure”, I said.

She grabbed my hand and we went outside together. We smoked and I started laughing because I wanted her to ask me what I was laughing about.

“This above all to thine own self be true”, I mumbled.

“What?” she asked.

“Oh it’s just a Shakespeare quote that popped into my head”, I said.

I exhaled smoke into the night. I sort of did feel smart what with the Shakespeare quote and the slight buzz I had going. Maybe she wanted me to kiss her but one of her friends came outside to get us. We went back inside and they went for a dance while I had a conversation with the others.

“Yes”, I said. “There’s a theme, a thematic thread that runs through our lives that we return to again and again.”

“Bullshit”, someone said. “Shit just happens to people and then we try to impose a theme on the shit that happens.”

“Well yes, otherwise what would it all mean? And if you think of it in terms of literature—“

"Are you saying the most meaningful lives have a theme running through them?"

"I'm not saying anything", I said, losing my way.

The girls came back from their dance and said they were going to another place to get something to eat. They wanted me to go with them. I looked at my watch.

"I have to go", I said.

My smoking partner hugged me. I couldn't remember her name but her hair smelled good. I took the smell home with me. I took it to the kitchen. I took it to the bathroom. I took it to bed. I stayed awake and pretended to be sleeping when Fever got home. She finally walked in and "woke me up". She said that she saw some of my friends at the club. She said she danced with one of them (just one?). I didn't ask who. But whoever it was, he was probably at home lying in bed remembering what Fever smelled like.

V

The next evening I felt as if what happened earlier that morning with the detectives was surreal or that it had happened a long time ago—that the memory of it crossed afternoon like it had travelled overnight across the Atlantic.

"You've heard about the missing boy?"

"Yes", I said.

"We're interviewing everyone on this street. Does anyone else live here?"

I felt the seriousness of the situation for the first time—the despair and grief that the boy's parents were feeling. Or I tried to feel it. I thought I did. But I also felt like a suspect standing in front of the two detectives. In fact, I wanted to feel like a suspect. While the detectives talked I imagined that the boy was hiding upstairs in our house somewhere. I was glad that I had paid attention to the news earlier. I was glad that Fever cried about it. It gave me something to tell the police.

"No, my girlfriend lives here also. We saw it on the news this morning. She couldn't stop crying."

"Did you cry?" one of them asked.

"Uhm, no", I said. "Well, maybe I felt like crying. I still might."

"Did you hear any noises outside or see anything out of the ordinary around dusk?" the second detective asked.

The word vespertine popped into my head.

(vespertine – of or relating to the evening)

"No", I said. "I thought he disappeared in the morning."

"Why do you think that?" he asked.

"No it's just that I saw on the news that his father said the last time they saw him was in the morning."

"We haven't made that determination yet", he said. "Did you know the boy or ever come into contact or have reason to come into contact with him?"

"No, I didn't know him", I said. "I'd see him every once in a while when he was riding his bike but I didn't know him. I said hello to his father once."

"Okay", he said. "Don't forget that we'd like to talk to your girlfriend also."

"She'll be back later this afternoon", I said. "Do you think he's going to be okay?"

I felt something that I considered to be *the-welling-up-of-tears* forming behind my eyes but they weren't real and the detectives would probably have been able to detect their falseness. I thought I had time to make them real before they walked away but I was wrong. So the detectives left without ever seeing me sad.

vi

I tell myself I'm a good person and then I look back on my day, my week, my month, to see if the facts actually support my assertion. It's easy enough to figure it out I think. Did I do good things? Did I help people who needed help? Was I unselfish? Did I do no wrong? And I check them off. But somewhere along the way, my intentions intrude. I have evil thoughts. Thoughts I'll never talk about or write down.

If the boy was hiding upstairs in our house he would enjoy himself. We have hardwood floors up there and an extra room. There's another bathroom in the hallway that he could use. I have two guitars I don't play. He could tune them.

He could wander around up there like he was floating. Move from room to room. Stand at the top of the stairs and look down on us when we were leaving. Maybe I'd be wrongly implicated because people would think I abducted him. The neighbors would see me getting arrested, see the television cameras and reporters, see the police pushing my head down as they forced me into the police car.

But that wouldn't feel so terrible would it? Being wrongly implicated, hated by neighbors, avoided by friends, only in the end to be vindicated.

vii

Fever came into the house yelling my name.

"Did you see the back of the house?"

"No", I said.

"Come here."

I followed her outside to the backyard.

"Look at the graffiti", she said. "Look at it."

The word "amputake" was spray painted with red paint on the white aluminum siding on the back of the house. I looked over to the house behind ours where the two brothers lived but I didn't think they were responsible. I thought they were good kids. I only looked over there because I wanted to act vaguely suspicious about someone and make it seem like I cared about the actual *graffiti-ing* of a house we didn't own.

"It's probably those two brothers", she said.

"Why would you say that?" I asked.

"Well, you need to go talk to their parents", she said.

"And tell them what?"

"Tell them that somebody spray-painted our house", she said. "I don't know. Tell them something. Find out."

"We'll bring it up at your neighborhood watch meeting", I said.

"They can't even spell", she said.

I didn't think 'amputake' was a misspelling. The uncle said the boy liked making up new words. The kid was probably running around the neighborhood somewhere after all I thought. Maybe he's scared from all the trouble he's caused. He's probably starving. All the police sirens and TV trucks and cameras. I'd probably disappear for a good, long time too until I thought people forgot about me and then just show up like nothing happened.

"It is cleverish", I said. "Amputate, take. You know they almost go together. Taking something like an arm or—"

"You're so fucking annoying sometimes", she said.

I couldn't disagree with Fever. I even felt annoyed at myself. I wanted to punch myself on the side of my head, near the temple area, but I knew that would annoy Fever even more.

viii

I met Deaf at Café Hopeless on Friday afternoon. He was already in a conversation with the bartender about—well, I couldn't quite figure it out.

"What are you talking about?" I asked him.

"What?" he said. "Nothing. Eh, don't worry about that. Let's drink."

But I couldn't take the mystery. While we were sitting there talking about him, me, Fever, the missing boy, and pre-Glasnost St. Petersburg (Leningrad), I kept wondering about Deaf and the bartender. When Deaf went to the bathroom I asked her what they were talking about when I walked in.

"Nihilism", she said.

"What about it?" I asked.

I had an idea about what nihilism was. Basically: life's not worth living. At least that's what I thought. And it was just typical of Deaf to get into a conversation that I couldn't really be a part of.

(nihilism – the view that nothing exists or that existence or values are meaningless)

"He was saying that the way we as humans think is okay but it's the world that's fucked up and I was saying that the world is okay but the way that we as humans think is fucked up."

I pondered the distinction but all I could think about was that I knew two people who disagreed on a fundamental philosophy of life but who would end up naked together in bed anyway.

"To thine own self be true", I said.

"More like hope in reality is the worst of all evils because it prolongs the torments of man", she said.

Her nostrils flared slightly when she spoke.

"Shakespeare", I mumbled, half-hoping she wouldn't hear me.

"Nietzsche", she said.

Of course. Look, I didn't care what Nietzsche said and I wasn't sure I liked the bartender. Maybe *her* thinking was fucked up. I tried to sort it out in my head before Deaf returned and felt that I fell into the first camp. I felt that my thinking was okay and it was the world that was fucked up. But the rest of the world was filled with other people's thinking so maybe the world was fucked up because of the way people were thinking. I'd never figure it out.

Still, it bothered me that Deaf didn't discuss nihilism with *me*. Maybe he knew I didn't have a good understanding of it and felt it was pointless (which is ironic right?). And yeah, I didn't know any Nietzsche quotes. But it still stung ever so slightly. Deaf returned and we kept drinking. I told him about the neighborhood watch meeting that Fever wanted me to go to with her.

"What? A neighborhood watch meeting on a Friday night?" he said.

“Yeah, that’s what I said”, I said.

“We should have two more shots and show up.”

I knew he was serious. But I also knew if we had three more shots he would change his mind.

“If I show up drunk Fever will be fucking furious”, I said.

“What?” he said. “Come on. She’ll be happy to see you take an interest. Then all three of us can go out afterwards and drink some more.”

“This world is fucked up”, I said. “Who’d fucking hurt a kid?”

“It’s fucked up alright”, Deaf said. “But there’s nowhere else to go.”

“Yeah”, I said. “The fucking evil torments of man.”

ix

The missing boy made me think about lost memories, which isn’t easy to do. The memories are lost so I end up asking myself *what am I really thinking about here*?

It was Saturday morning. The night after the neighborhood watch meeting, the night after Deaf and I went drinking. I should have been in bed sleeping it off. But Fever dragged me out for a "promenade" even though I told her I wasn't feeling well. She wasn't happy with me but the weirdness at the neighborhood watch meeting wasn't all my fault. I told her I had to sit down somewhere and try to eat some breakfast. She left me at a diner and went on her promenade without me.

While I stared at my plate of eggs and bacon, a woman sat down with her plate of waffles at a table across from me. She was mesmerizing. Even surrounded by the meandering of people taking their morning blinkers off, the noisy clinking and clanking of forks, knives, cups, plates and the everyday indecency of dripping syrup and bits of fallen bacon, she was the personification of grace. The way she cut her waffles, pried (ever so gently) into the pieces with her fork (she used the small one), and raised them to her freshly washed lips (pink, soft, and slightly damp in the best way).

I couldn't take my eyes off of her. And for a moment here or there our eyes would meet and then we would look away. I felt that this was what life was all about—making connections. Even in the smallest possible way. Perhaps we had come to some primordial understanding that went back to the dawn of humanity. Our eyes met again. There was an air about her. Or she changed the air that existed about her—made it more meaningful. She leaned over her plate of waffles and whispered to me.

"Stop staring at me you fucking creep."

I looked around to see if anyone noticed. I was deeply wounded but moved on to a word I saw written on the wall beside her: “burble”. Maybe the missing boy was leaving messages for me to find. Trying to make a connection in the smallest possible way—syllable by syllable.

The woman got up and left. She looked at me and shook her head as if I were exactly what she had called me. She didn’t seem so graceful anymore. Could she imagine me speaking to the boy in the same way she spoke to me? The boy was missing. Were those the words to say to a fellow human being at such a time? Maybe that was her way of making a primordial connection. We were connected now anyway. She made sure of that.

Part 2

S{E}AN? THINKS

tropics

I was always comfortable with the idea of death in the tropics. Not so much in colder climes. But I became accustomed to death's idea in those places as well. My journey with death started early. In the country I was born, near the house I lived in, until my first death. It wasn't the ocean but it came from the ocean. The ocean that brought all of death that had ever sunk beneath it on the air it carried onto land. One moment we are here. Then we are not. And everything goes on as it will.

ocean

The ocean is not an ocean. It is a body of water that meets the land. But it is an ocean. The horses and dogs that run wild on the thin strip of land before the rocks have permission from the earth. But we also have permission. We also have muscle. Not as strong or as sinewy as the nobler animals but with the same kinetic desires. And so we run, my sister and I, from the gate of our house to the beach while the youngest in our family sleeps within the mosquito net, beneath the fan, the hum of which synthesizes the sounds of chickens and goats coming from the yard outside our house so that this family's youngest, this young boy we call brother, may sleep in good time.

My sister and I run with new muscle and bone that expand and stretch and push our bodies forward. We run in the air that comes from the ocean, from the water that meets the land—that flows over the noble animals and encourages us to carry on. We are as fast as they and soon move among them until I stumble and hear the wind and the water and the hammering of hooves around me. This was my first death.

planes

I have always had evil thoughts. I am afraid to speak about them or write them down. I think about what I might do to people who are standing in line with me at the grocer's. I put my legumes and wild fish down. I raise the cutlass I hold in my hand. The cashier smiles before I bring it down on his wrist. But I am not there yet. I am only six. I hide the toy airplane in my pocket. I have pulled it loose from its package.

I see my mother further down the aisle. She is a good mother. She takes care of her children—her children who have come so far to be with her. But I am stealing. She has never taught me this. It was my desire. I will take this airplane and walk out of the store with it. Perhaps I had other desires before this one but I can't remember them. This was my strongest desire.

I take the airplane to school and push it across my desk while the teacher talks about subtraction. Yes Mrs. Pear, I subtracted this airplane from the store. I understand. Sathan has his eyes on my airplane. I think Sathan also knows about subtraction. We will become friends because we recognize in each other this gift for subtraction. Perhaps our friendship will last.

blood

I don't know about the studies of reality, existence, and time—the relationship between what is inside and what is outside. About what is real and whether that reality is constructed by the mind or independent of it. Perhaps we are born good. But in time we learn to see evil at the bottom of the stairs. We run in the cold with our friends, our winter hats loosening from our heads, then falling off. Shall we find them before we go home? Our parents will be angry that we have lost them. We run wild but there is no other way to fight this evil. We stay in motion. We move and spit. We roll on the ground and give up our skin to the cold gravel. Little pieces scraped off by the rough. Infinitesimal splotches of blood injected into the ruts. One day an animal will walk through this space, lean down, and sniff at the microscopic remnants of skin and blood we have left behind.

sun

I remember the summer and the sun during this time. The light from above. The iron gates and wooden benches. And you and him. How happy as the tree behind you shimmered. He picked you up and you held around him. Why couldn't you be mine? I am older here. I can imagine the feeling. To hold this type of beauty. To pick you up and pull you into my chest. Maybe you were unhappy some time. Maybe it wouldn't last. But not at this moment. This moment that was yours was always around me.

What is London? Or Berlin? Or Athens? Up there it is the tower and the wall and the acropolis. Down here it is the small room, the water in the street, the voice of a friend calling behind you when you have gone outside to be sick. Even Moscow returns to the small flat you grew up in where you knock on the door and the girl still combing her hair answers and the boy with a toothbrush in his mouth stares through the curtains.

one

There are many reasons one might disappear, not the least of which is that one wants to disappear. Wanting to disappear is the first reason to think of when one disappears. Perhaps one is poisoned and buried beneath a tree. But the storm uproots the tree and with it the poisoned body.

If one were cut to pieces, a part of one might still be found by a dog or a wolf and carried to a nearby village. If one were drowned one might float up in the net of a fisherman. If one climbed to the top of a crane to live out one's life one might succumb to weariness and fall to the ground. And again one would be found.

iron

I think about what he's thinking about but I'm also thinking about the *amputaken* ear. Like Var Gaul (Van Gogh) who painted his last painting with his *amputaken* ear and the tiny hairs still stuck to the lobe. They found his favorite yellow on the cilia.

evil

I disappear to fight evil but sometimes the evil consumes me.

fire

I remember hands clapping as we alight. My mother taking us to the park for a Sunday picnic. I'm watching my sister and brother from the tree. Around us I make a circle of fire and make sure that it's warm on the inside so we don't get burned. I make the fire hot on the outside so that evil-doers are burned when they come near us. And they do come near us. Fire attracts evil-doers and burns them at the same time.

i-give-it-all-to-you

These are all of my creations.

Part 3

S{E}AN? READS

café hopeless

I'm not sure if anyone showed up to watch me read at Café Hopeless on Saturday evening but here are some pictures from the event. I sat in a comfortable chair in the corner of the first floor parlor. I ordered a coffee (black) and waited until it arrived to start reading. I read all of A and B from my dictionary. In this picture I'm reading "ableberry". I took a break afterwards to drink my coffee and think about what I was thinking about when I wrote "ableberry". I have no idea.

I looked out the window for a few minutes and I thought I saw someone I knew looking back at me. Maybe she was there to watch me read and decided to watch me from outside the café.

I got more comfortable and really started reading. By the time I put my leg over the chair I had whoever might be there to watch me read riveted. I looked over the book a few times and noticed that only a few people left the café while I was reading. I know what you're thinking—putting my leg over the chair was bad form but it was for the sake of art. I was overcome by the text and let myself go. Poetry has that kind of effect on me and I don't think I should apologize for that. I chuckled a few times while I was reading B because I remembered what a reviewer wrote about B: "utter nonsense". I bet you he wishes he was there at Café Hopeless on September 28, 2014. Too bad for him.

Here I'm finishing my coffee. I probably shouldn't have had any because later that night I had a difficult time falling asleep and missed some dreaming. When I finished reading I noticed people staring at me. Maybe they wanted me to read some more. I don't know. By the way, I read for myself and the people who watch me read. I wore my favorite shoes for this reading. I don't wear them often but they're still my favorite.

<u>what i was reading at café hopeless on 9/28</u>

A

ableberry

and lo there goes my father [she's singing] stop staring. irretrievable the floor vanished. and for only me {she} carried my body to the strafe.

Underneath the glass she looks the same but her hair is different. I remember the smell of her room and the window barely opened looking down onto the small yard and how the breeze lifted her drawings from the wall. When she returned I would hear her bicycle rattle against the tree, the front door open and close, and her hurried footsteps getting nearer to our room. I always thought to myself and sometimes whispered: 'be careful on the stairs'. That's how much I loved her.

the degas room

I arrived at the Degas Room earlier than 8 p.m. because I heard through a friend there was another event taking place at the same time I was scheduled to read there. When I arrived I was told I had to pay to get in. I told them that I was there to read. They said they couldn't help me. There was an event taking place at the Degas Room and I wasn't allowed in without paying. So I stood in the entrance and decided I would read right there and let the people walking into the Degas Room watch me while I was reading.

The man at the entrance told me I had to take off my hat. I was surprised because I've never heard of an art gallery that didn't allow hats. I told the man that if he'd ever been to an art gallery that didn't allow hats I'd like to know about it. I told him I only wanted to read—silently, peacefully. I tried to block him out (be in the now) but I didn't get very far. My biographer (Maria) snapped this photograph of me before we were escorted out of the entrance of the Degas Room. I only read the beginning of "dreams of terrible angels". I can't be sure if anyone watched me reading.

Below is a photograph of me reading out loud at another art gallery that did allow hats even though I wasn't wearing one.

what i was reading at the degas room on 10/02:

D

dreams of terrible angels

two lovers in the snow. Two lovers framed by jade (color). Two lovers pierced by the sword of a mighty rhododendron (flower).

the karl marx klub

The Karl Marx cenotaph outside the Karl Marx Klub was always being peed on. The message scrawled on it read "go back to Russia" (Russia? хи хи). The Klub owners liked to think of the Klub as the most subversive meeting place in America but the two times I had been there I didn't see much subversion. In fact, one night I was there, there was a members-only karaoke contest. I had to leave at 10 p.m. when the singing started. The only other time I had been there was when my last book *The Unknowed Things* was published back in 2009. I put it on my list of places to read on my current reading tour. Unfortunately, the Karl Marx Klub had closed down. The closing was unexpected. One story was that the owner moved back to Vermont to be closer to his children. Another story was that he needed to make more money. The place was still being packed up—there were boxes everywhere—so I decided to read in there for a little while before the doors closed for good (one last time). I sat down on the floor and got comfortable against a few of the boxes and read for a few minutes before the movers asked me to get out of their way. I suppose they did watch me read while they were shuffling in and out.

what i was reading at the karl marx klub on 10/05:

F

feeltrip

what mendacity is this that proclaimed itself thus upon my bereavement? It is a cold bluster of mind that turns to keep a man's soul from ascent.

This is the way of Marstrand—passing five sins to Marga^re|t. She is of consequence in her plastic arcade. Some whisper in search of favorite colors and numbers and I am that boy. Someone made the cave. Someone made the footpath to the slave. Someone made the slave. It was all still and then she flew. In the cave pictures of new animals (they say we were almost apart).

There is a noise that reminds me of my loss. Those missing on the ferry to Marstrand. The walk by the water and rocks. The fell. My loss saved in half bubbles floating in puddles of rain. The boats painted [yellow and blue] with ropes drifting out to the boy.

I am entering now. The place. The skin beneath her skin that I touch (more than touch, more than skin) in the room above the sea where the bones of men mingle with those of animals.

the noontz

Years ago The Noontz was one of my favorite places to go because not only was The Noontz itself a place to go but there was a place to go inside The Noontz that most people didn't know about. There was a room behind the coat room that we would slip into through a half-door behind the coats. We called this room "The Room" as in see you in the room. This room shared a wall with one of the smaller bars inside the Noontz. On that wall was a small window that opened and closed (we usually kept it open) through which we received our nightly fuel. The Noontz is still open but new owners have walled over the half-door that led to The Room behind the coat room. There was nothing fancy about The Room—no talking lions or witches—but we felt as if we were each "one of the living" while we were in there. The feeling was good anyway.

The first time I went into The Noontz someone introduced himself to me as Archie (nickname for Artto he said) and showed me a long knife he kept in his jacket. He told me he had enemies in there (he pointed them out to me), that he collected stamps, and that if I wanted to meet his girlfriend that was okay with him. I remember telling him that maybe it wasn't safe for him to be there but he said he'd be okay as long as he was talking to a neutral. He said there was some Nietzsche v. Hegel thing going on in the city and that he was a Nietzsche boy (even though his girlfriend was a Hegel girl) and The Noontz was Hegel territory. He told me not to be fooled by his gang clothing because he graduated from university with a Botany degree. After a few drinks he said he had to leave but wanted me to walk to the exit with him and possibly further. So I walked to the exit with him but I couldn't leave because I was waiting for someone else. It was after he rode off on his motorcycle and I turned around to go back into The Noontz that I saw someone slip into what later became known to me as The Room. After going to The Noontz a few more times and talking to the coat girl I was allowed to go into The Room whenever I wanted. The Room didn't last long—

maybe eight months—but, like most things, it was better that way.

There are many stories to tell about The Room and what happened there but those types of stories damage easily from explanation, so best for me to leave them untold.

My biographer Maria took a couple of photographs of me reading in the coat room. The owners allowed me to read there as long as I blended into the coats (therefore the coat-like flannel hoodie) so as not to turn away their patrons (who actually watched me read without knowing that they were).

what i was reading at the noontz on 10/08:

J

jespertine

gone good are days of long and lonely suffering when the window shingles (fermata, algernon, and caribou) conspire with words like reckon or dragoon master willister to confound us.

Ours was the house seen from the road. But only the back door and the bedroom window above, framed by trees on either side. If you had a pretty dress mother or one moment to rest upon the stairs I would have told you that not far from here I impressed a girl by saying: 'the trumpet is the most beautiful sculpture I've ever seen'.

the yellow bookshop

The Yellow Bookshop collides (aesthetically) with all of the other shops on Kalorama Road. It is the only shop on the road that one might live above and look out through a window to the street below. The window, of course, would frost over during the night and wouldn't do much to keep out the cold. But the next morning a young man might draw the outline of a small circle on the frosted glass and then wipe clear the circle inside the outline in order to see through the window and there spy, perfectly framed by the transparent disc, the face of a woman—a woman he might see on the street as he walked home (his hands filled with groceries) and who knew nothing of him other than he had said hello to her once as he walked by her.

I have bought over 500 books from The Yellow Bookshop. Here is a list of some of them:

- The Life and Opinions of Tristram Shandy, Gentleman
- The Sleepwalkers
- Ferdydurke
- The Count of Monte Christo
- Juliette
- Jenseits von Gut und Böse: Vorspiel einer Philosophie der Zukunft
- Thus Spoke Zarathustra
- The Antichrist
- Hedda Gabler
- If On a Winter's Night a Traveler
- Invitation to a Beheading

- The Castle
- Madame Bovary
- Le Rouge et le Noir
- The Sun Also Rises
- The Complete Poems of Anna Akhmatova
- Their Eyes Were Watching God
- The Rubaiyat of Omar Khayyam
- Autumn of the Patriarch
- Life is Elsewhere
- Don Quixote
- Tractatus Logico-Philosophicus
- Light in August
- The Book of Imaginary Beings
- The Street of Crocodiles
- The Man Who Was Thursday

The Yellow Bookshop is closed now so I was not able to read there.

<u>what i would have read at the yellow bookshop on 10/10:</u>

E

evil of goodness

this dream-like sequence, the basis of all conversation, is an example of a near-perfect combination of form and function. It provides an environment in which people can exist [live]. Rules are established of what can or should be said and of what cannot or should not be said. In turn, expectations are met, practice is rewarded, and humans may interact in relative safety.

We're on a ship that's sinking and you and I move away from where the water's filling. They'll bring a fire truck on deck to put out the fire. It's a long ship and there's lots of space. But we'll have to jump over. Near the ship there's a pond and we see pond things while we're swimming underneath. Storybook pond things that invert words like vespertine (from the viny) or crepuscular just for this sense. It looks like an old city but it's just an old town. And when the Indian sailors come rowing over to tell us how they fixed her up, we'll tell them to row back because we'll be staying here a while. We'll say 'you'll find us waiting here M+ati/lda, our sweat collecting in the creases of a bamboo porch.'

It could be the land of turtles or the land of underneath water. But we are a relevant species, scraping chum along the briny, humming jingles while flowers bloom from the bottom of our shoes.

sixth and i historic

"you win by a petal. your prize is the flower."

I saw you sing at *sixth and i historic*. I didn't rush to the front like the others but waited for the hall to fill before I found my place in the back. Quietly, as you introduced your next song, I turned to a passage in my book that moved in near perfect harmony with your melody. You improvised your introduction but I matched you with an improvisation of my own—reading as if my English were tinged with the accent of *la isla de Madeira*. When the song finished I stopped reading and then I saw something I could never have imagined—a woman in the back of the hall reading a book (as I was). I watched her throughout the night and noticed that she only read between songs—during the pauses, while I read as you sang. She never saw me but I wanted her to see me. I would read for a few moments and then look up to see if she was looking at me but she never did. When it was time for everyone to leave I tried to find her in the crowd but she was gone.

<u>what i was reading at sixth and i historic on 11/09/2013:</u>

The Epilogue

from the Arch-Enemies Handbook

It is with good intentions that I wish for everyone an arch-enemy. But not everyone is predisposed to or capable of living with an arch-enemy. "living with" as in existing on the same planet at the same time. Arch-enemies can be imagined and/or non-reciprocating. These types of arch-enemies, however, do not allow us to develop the powers necessary for combating our real arch-enemies. Imagined or non-reciprocating arch-enemies are good practice but everyone (in good time) needs the power of a real arch-enemy to endure and eventually overcome.

It was in second grade that I developed my first real arch-enemy: Sathan. It was this relationship that provided the arc and structure of my subsequent arch-enemy relationships.

Sathan and I were good friends at the beginning of the school year but by the third quarter, due to some real or perceived injustice (any slight will do) we had become true and committed arch-enemies. A good friend is the best candidate for a future arch-enemy and by becoming one and opposing you, bestows upon you the greatest honor any friend ever could.

my hand (right)

lecture hall fc

Lecture Hall FC also known as The Saints is over 300 years old. It stands not far from the bank of the Zala River, separated from the water, by a busy road and a row of small lemon trees. I cannot enter The Saints because readings are by invitation only. Instead I sat on its steps and watched the moored boats and canoes bob up and down as cars passed by. On the other side of the river—perhaps I was not seeing clearly—I saw the woman I watched read at *6th and I historic.* She was walking with a

book in her hand. So many weeks later—to see her again—to see her reading again. I thought it was more than coincidence. I watched her better today. In the light. Though I couldn't make out the book she was reading. But she surprised me by looking in my direction. I became nervous for no reason and opened a booklet about the history of The Saints that was folded in my hand. I read from that booklet as if I were reading from the most beautiful book ever written. I studied its folded and frayed pages; I lingered on the sounds the words formed in my brain, on the shapes of the letters. I thought about how they tried to live for me, about how together they and I moved towards the understanding that while we were all frayed and coming further apart, that we were coming apart together, and that we could spend what little time we had in each other's company without fuss and perhaps even pleasantly.

<u>what i was reading on the steps of the saints 11/28/2013:</u>

from Gounot's A Guide to The Dictionary of Coincidences Machine lecture

Sartre's idea of a Dictionary of Coincidences Machine has been studied by both philosophers and neuroscientists since he broached the subject at the historic Lecture Hall FC. And while poets have postulated about the machine, Gounot suggests that their postulations are nothing more than hagiography to the Machine, its creator, and the postulations themselves. Nonetheless, Gounot believes that the interpretations of Sartre's original concept by poets are advantageously misguided and reveal the variability of the Machine and its capacity for absorbing, mutating, regenerating, and creating neural pathways in human beings. Neuroscientists have cautioned poets to stay out of the scientific debate vis-à-vis the Machine and to focus instead on the Machine's "cortical" effects. But Gounot, in his own landmark lecture at The Saints, cautioned neuroscientists to stay out of poetry.

central library

I've started regarding myself as someone who is learned. Not educated or intelligent but learned. So I took my book with me to a nearby university campus and sat on the base of a column of the central university library. Central is what I think they call these libraries that are at the center of institutions where one might become learned or at least where some amount of the contagion that is learnedness might be caught, cultured, and spread throughout the body. While I sat and read my book it began to rain and the students who I would have considered 'passers-by' in one of the following sentences had it not rained began to huddle beneath the shelter provided by the library (a metaphor for learnedness if there ever was one).

I became distracted by the feeling that something had gotten a hold of me. My mind started to remind itself of previous interests—Goethe, Nietzsche, Wittgenstein, Stendhal—and then it delved even further to understand what made it remind itself of its previous interests—

restlessness, boredom, dissatisfaction—and then even further to understand why restless, why bored, why dissatisfied—and then even further to understand why it needed to understand why. And then I saw the woman who I saw at *6th and i historic* (if only briefly) and who interrupted my delving (and further interrupted my reading), pass through the crowd of students who had begun to disperse as the rain let up. She departed into that institution of learnedness (learnedness is a departure with no arrival) and I thought it was not possible that we could ever meet so long as I desired to be learned. But I desired to be learned and accepted the fact that she and I could only ever meet as two people passing by each other (possibly unaware of this passing) from time to time as we made our way along our separate paths.

<u>**what i was reading at central library 2/28/2014:**</u>

rememory

Starting with the trees. Starting with the path leading to the trees. The trees were tall in the forest. She turned to look back. Slowly mon ami. And the leaves? They fell did they not? So many. So many fell around her. And then she turned again. Slowly. My god she turned. So slowly, so full of grace, that we mistook her for air.

It's no small feat to make one's way. It requires an understanding of the metaphysics between one's self and the objects that orbit one's self. It would have been no surprise to Molly and her objugates if she had awakened one morning and wished for a kind of normal that comes without explanations. But Molly's normal came with an urgent request for the revolver.

(pop)

(pop) (pop-pop)

(pop) (pop)

(pop-pop) (pop)

the burble lounge

The Burble Lounge was a place I didn't like to go to but I had friends who admired the posh setting and elevated ambience. I decided that even though I didn't like the setting or ambience that I would still go to read there—to sit in one of the lounge's posh, elevated chairs, sip a whiskey, and read from my book. People would notice. Or so I thought. But when I was there a group of people sitting around one of the chic burble tables had drawn everyone's attention. They were taking photographs of themselves.

I thought about photographs and of how the photographs that some people take make their life look better than mine. But I think in real life that my life is just as good as theirs.

[And so I watch the friends around the table. Ba$r%b7ara's legs fall over D#ieg3o's legs. D#ieg2o has almost disappeared into the sofa while Car9m^en has her arms around Ro44ger's waist and P!au#l has his arm around Am$%ber. Lil7y and Fr36anc4esca hug and smile. They all have drinks in their hands, laughing and waving to the camera. But in that moment after the photograph was taken, Ro55ger became angry because he saw P^a+ul's hand against Am4*ber's ass and Am44ber smiled (meaning she liked it). At the very moment after Herm3ione said *continuar a sorrir* and pressed the button on the camera, words were spoken, friends were lost, and lives were destroyed forever.]

The group gathered around. Everyone smiled and the photograph was taken. I read from my book of essays as one or two from the group watched me very (very) closely. I reflected on the woman from *6th and i historic* while I read. She was not *Beth* but *Beth Singular.*

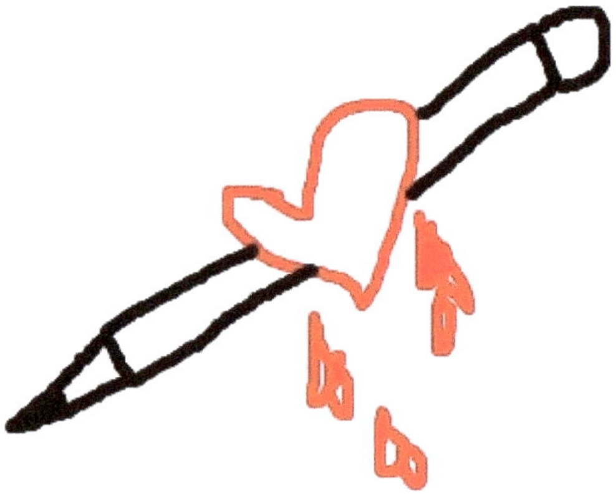

what i was reading at the Burble Lounge 4/6/2014

Beth or Beth singular

For Beth, who one finds but is never there, the crowd is invisible. No matter how distracted or preoccupied or late we are in looking when at last we look our eyes fall immediately upon her and no one else. At the most obscure angles and bend of our neck we find her. In the most uneasy and unexpected circumstances we find her. She is never beside us before we find her and then we wait or meet her halfway and while we are waiting or meeting her halfway we feel the breeze on our face and we are overcome by a feeling of happiness.

For Beth Singular who is always there before we find her, the crowd is never small enough. If she were to walk hand in hand with just one other human being along a path framed by (let us say) pear trees on either side she would be obscured by the shade of a single leaf. We think we see her but—refocusing—we see that it is not her. It is the shadow of a passing sparrow or a loose strand of someone's tightly clasped hair (and we wonder if it is hers). We lament that we cannot find her like we find Beth. We endeavor and while we endeavor she is suddenly there beside us. We never see her before she is there. And when she is there we feel the breeze on our face and we are overcome by a feeling of happiness.

And so we ponder the very real possibility of not finding Beth or of Beth Singular not being there. We are filled with dread. We don't understand the configurations of a life that brought us to this—the entanglement of the relationship we have with each. We cannot make sense of why this is so and we worry that to delve too far into either would be to shake loose the tightly woven but delicate threads that bring them to us in their own way. We think that one day we will understand. Not because we are thoughtful or inspired but because the reason will simply become clear to us.

ginny's juke joint

In this world no thought is alone. Of the nine billion people living on the planet there will always be one other person thinking exactly what you are thinking at exactly the same moment. Maybe in different words or images but there will always be at least one.

The woman from *6th and i historic* and I were theoretically having the same thought in almost the same words. But why didn't she watch me read? We were both reading at *6th and i* but she didn't notice. I had to find out what she was reading. I could read it also. If I was reading the same book that she was reading she would probably notice me.

A boy sitting at the table next to me drew on a napkin:

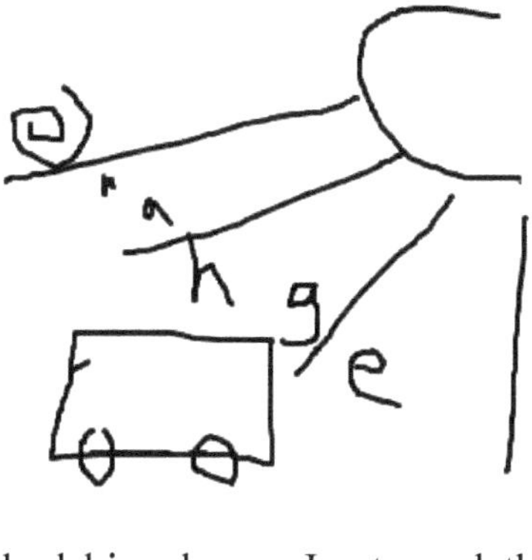

I watched him draw. I returned the favor and started reading. I saw him watching me. I read carefully, gently, without menace so the little boy would not be afraid.

<u>what i was reading at ginny's juke joint 5/2/2014</u>

a drawing of sweet serenade

The first snow of winter arrives before winter but not enough to reach the outstretched hand of the girl looking up to the sky. Where does this winter come from? She thinks not the sky but if not from the sky then from the sea. Then the snow. Heavy and slow. It brings cold through the glass. It brings another winter. From another room I hear the sound of a broom sweeping against the floor. Someone has made tea and started a fire in the small fireplace. From here I remember the three chairs (each its own color) and table in the center that our forefathers could never have imagined.

In front of me there is window through which one might see the snow falling and the snow that has fallen. The snow that reaches up to the ledge and that will (in time) overcome this small house.

meridian hill park

I returned to Meridian Hill Park to see that the iron gates were gone. I thought back to the summer and the sun during that time and conceded that the moment that was yours was no longer around me. But the woman from *6th and i* had given me hope.

I opened my book and started reading. A man playing chess moved one of his pieces and turned to watch me read.

<u>what i was reading at meridian park 6/17/2014</u>

SEQUENCE DISRUPTOR 8

dear s{e}an?,

when we are old we must save play for the young. surrender it in shame and in shame accept their ridicule. we must walk the garden of serpents and feel their animal blood in our spine. we must go blind and die before we reach the end. that is our end. who would be reproached for thinking that such a creature could ever inspire awe? and yet *we* are awed. here in our face, tall ships cross the sea and descend into the vitreous.

(love always (love always (love always,
e{m}ma+

the cemetery near the tractor club

The world around the cemetery became modern but the cemetery remained old. The Tractor Club was built near it and flashed neon on the headstones at night. I went there to read because I wanted both the living and the dead to watch me read.

I talked to them to let them know that I was afraid of them—that I was afraid of dying even though sometimes I thought they were in a better place than most people living in the world.

I read the names and dates on the headstones. The young ones made me sad. In a cemetery as in the apartment building across the street one can find people of all ages.

<u>what i was reading at the cemetery 7/12/2014:</u>

subtraction ii

i pass the time
with our lesser demons Verrier and
the purveyor of good company Olivier
while above us the nimbost-on-strati
drifts and drifts and drifts
because *le sturm liebe Freunde*
bist kommer

Part 4

S{E}AN? WRITES

a semi-critique of pneumania by burton carl

Thesis: don't tell anyone about your skills if a girl who has a boyfriend is listening.

Pneumania is a touching tale of a boy wandering the big city hoping to find someone to beat up because he doesn't know how to play the trumpet. He likes a girl who likes parrots but he doesn't like parrots which makes it mathematically impossible for the girl to like him back. But the boy is unaware of this arithmetic which makes his plight all the more tragic. In the end the boy does find someone to play board games with which makes his life bearable. And for that we may thank our sympathetic writer.

This story was originally published in Bookman Old Style font which added just enough tenderness to the telling to make the story resonate in this reader's eyes. The narrator encapsulates the forlorn, passive anxiety of his (?) generation—a generation that improbably "looks to the stars for answers to the sea". The writing, though concise and tight, is surprisingly careless. Don't ask me how this can be. But the story is filled with the kind of flint that just might spark the docile mind. Passages lean toward the didactic but thankfully never quite fall over. (By the way, I look exactly like that and don't forget to buy men's clothing.)

-- *Burton Carl*

from
"One Note Symphonies"

PNEUMANIA

upstairs in her bedroom

The bed is unmade and I see a long strand of hair on her pillow.

"Those aren't lions," she says.

I watch her lift her arms to the ceiling to touch them. There is something soft in her--something that smells like spring blossoms. And she blossoms before me slowly. So slowly, that I think the universe desires her too and causes the rain that suddenly begins to fall.

music and flying

There is a relationship between music and flying that has yet to be studied. For example, how the arc of a crow's flight influences the texture of a Beethoven sonata. Or how the delicate shifts of a pigeon's wing effects cadence in a Mahler symphony or a Janacek concerto.

In fact, just the other day, Ravel's Bolero was irrevocably changed by the diving of a clumsy pelican.

the bicycle in the yard

The bicycle in the yard is getting wet. The clouds sweep away the blue sky, and she is sleeping.

"I want to tell you something while you are sleeping," I say, "I want to tell you that something has changed. No one can know. The flow of things has changed. This room is different. There is a tension. A feeling, after all. A tension that I want to speak about. A captivating, tangible—yet intangible, movement of some sort. A gripping dementia. A dense impression. A something."

She turns over on her side and wraps the white blanket around her body. The rain falls harder and I imagine her riding a wet bicycle.

"Don't think of things like that," she says, "I don't want to get pneumonia."

java

"Pneumonia", she says.

Smoke drifts between us, and I wait for a sign--a sea to part, a door to open, a leg to spread.

"Would you like to smell my java?" she asks (I hear a dog barking).

The trumpet player smiles at her when he plays. She smiles back at him. And then I say the unspeakable. Three words that are forced out of my gullet by a geyser of intense emotion. Three words that set me on a course of a subtle, but draining self deceit: "I hate jazz".

And so I resist the temptation to tap my feet, or to snap my fingers. I sigh. I yawn. I look away and search for the deepest, darkest, most defiled labyrinth of my soul.

friedrich nietzsche and sherlock holmes

"The degree and kind of a man's sexuality reach up into the ultimate pinnacle of his spirit."

So said a great philosopher and psychologist.

"What do you think that means?" she asks me.

"That is a vexed question", I say.

"Vexed indeed", she says, "there are no markings on the original Hung Wu."

It's raining harder, so we stop and wait in the doorway of a sex shop. She smokes a cigarette. In the shop window rubber penises and plastic women advertise themselves. Across the street, men wander in and out of a private sauna. But in the midst of this suggestive depravity, I try a pure and honest approach, because sometimes even the truth works.

"I like you very much", I tell her.

"I like the big, blue one", she says.

Bilingual prostitutes I think to myself. Are there any? But that's too simple. And then: is there more than one word that ends with the letter v? Down boy, down. Vexed indeed.

mediocrity

I have no talent. And therefore, I must make due with a common, mediocre soul. And to admit with the little sincerity I have and without pretension, that I desire a simple life and that I am profoundly happy with the little things that I have and with my place in the universe.

"It's not jazz", she says.

And so I ignore distinctions. I ignore the fact that the trumpet player is much more talented than I am. Or that I am slightly more talented than the man sitting at the next table. For me there is only genius or mediocrity.

“I’m a simple man”, I say, “I don’t understand the complexities and nuances of such an esoteric art.”

“I’m getting sleepy”, she says.

We leave the cafe’. It’s still raining and the darker circles of her body reveal themselves to me through her dress.

“The ability to make distinctions”, she says, “is a sign of intelligence.”

Ouch!

“What’s the matter?” she asks me.

“I hurt my foot”, I say.

the goose

Of all the birds that affect Chopin, in a positive or a negative way, the goose has the most profound influence. I was listening to Chopin’s Variations in B flat, Opus 2 on “La ci darem la mano”. Pre-goose, the instrumentation is sketchy at best, the flourishes fall flat, and the articulations are barely perceptible. With other birds, such as the falcon or the parrot the flourishes are lively, but again the instrumentation and overall orchestral quality of the piece disappoints. Only the swan and the duck ((male duck) as they are related) come close to effecting Chopin in the way that the goose does. However, only the goose with its long neck in flight, its webbed feet tucked back, and its grace as part of an entire flock (especially in a bright blue sky) transforms the piece into genius. Suddenly, the bewildering variety of articulation and flourishes are established. The tempest of triplet figurations and decorative variations become magnificent. And the cumulative virtuosity of the entire piece is made apparent to even the average listener.

only loved at night

I walk down Istedgade and a woman with bright, blonde hair approaches me.

"Do you want to go with me?" she asks.

"Yes", I say, "yes I do. But I won't."

I continue down the street as if I stumbled upon a crack on the sidewalk (looking back). A blue light shines on the horizon and a warm breeze blows on my face—a breeze I imagine originating from somewhere between her legs.

"On second thought", I say, "perhaps we could wager a few krones on a game of backgammon."
"How odd", she says walking towards me "because I prefer backgammon to chess."

“Is it because backgammon is more like life?” I inquire from the distance.

“Tie me up”, she says, still walking towards me, “yes. Things happen. Logical and illogical. Talent and chance combine. It is an ambiguous world where plans are made and abandoned, and man succumbs to the existential pressure that things beyond his control exert.”

“Indeed”, I say.

“And then there is you and me”, she says stopping in front of me, “you and me. Before money passes hands, and despite the lashes of chaos that strike at us, you and I must smile at the sadistic dominance of one over the other, even say motherly and fatherly words as we resign ourselves to the role of the victor and the vanquished.”

We go to her apartment, where I beat her for three hundred krones.

a mutiny at thermopylae

“If I do something amazing”, she says, “a hundred years from now when the story is told, it will be a fairy tale.”

The more she drifts away, the more grounded I become, the more concise my desires become. So concise, in fact, that when I speak, whether I speak about the collapse of the Danish empire or about the little boy who was almost run over by a car this morning, that what I want is no longer hidden—no longer protected from the formidable no. And so I retreat into a Thermopylae of silence.

However, there is something genuine about desperation, something that defies dishonesty (and silence). And like seamen trapped in the brig of some long barge, my desperation attempts to reach out beyond its purgatory.

“I can’t take it anymore!”, I scream, “Just give it up! Please! I’m begging you!”

“I think your coffee is too hot”, she says, “the glass is cracking.”

the dumbest bird in the world

“The trumpet”, she says, “is the most beautiful sculpture I’ve ever seen.”

The trumpet player smiles and I sigh.

“This is my pet parrot”, he says, “I call him Miles.”

Mother of God! I have yet to do research on parrots and jazz.

“Parrots are the dumbest birds in the world”, I say (I don’t know).

They shake their heads. Ah, the subtly Watson. Only the keenest eye could have detected that. They shake their heads together, and in the same way. I pretend that I don't notice.

"Do you want to come see my band play tonight?" he asks me.

"I don't have any money!"I shout, "I spent three hundred krones last night!"

the parrot and jazz

It is a commonly known fact that the three most important colors in jazz are red, yellow, and green. Red for bloodlessness. Yellow for cowardice. And green for greedy, grimy, grabbing bastards. And trumpet is similar to trumpery, which comes from tromper which means to deceive. And that's what those fucking parrots do.

the woman with bright, blonde hair

The Palae Bar is crowded, and I'm waiting in line. I see her and the trumpet player inside talking at the bar. The line moves a little. Now they're laughing, and the line moves a little bit more. The parrot is on his shoulder and she strokes it with her finger. Then the line stops. They're not letting any more people in. And so I stand outside the window of the Palae Bar (clawing, clawing). Not once does she look back. The band is playing and yes—now I do hate jazz.

I leave and walk towards Istedgade. I see a few girls riding their bicycles. It's still raining, and although I have no money, I'm searching for that woman with bright, blonde hair. Maybe tonight, she'll let me beat her for what little I have left.

a semi-critique of the unknowed things by vladimira (mira) oblonsky

Thesis: one epiphany can justify a mistaken life

the unknowed things is probably the shortest piece of writing that readers never finish reading. In that sense it is the War and Peace of work that is < 1500 words. I know five people who have started to read it but none of them ever made it to the end. Although one of those people said she actually read all of War and Peace.

The first paragraph of *the unknowed things* gave me nightmares for 3 days. I woke up wondering how anyone who didn't have those kinds of nightmares could put those words down on paper. It was more than just gashing and slashing or vampires and murderers. It was something far more sinister. The 'civilization paths' that S{E}AN? writes about can't be found anywhere in this piece and maybe that's the point. We are told that any 'perfume' of hope and possibility in this world comes from the 'royal stem'. It doesn't take an erudite reader to discern the meaning. But the blame isn't placed on any one individual/archetype or his/her royal stem.

For those who want to be one with the world and believe that meaning and the wonders of existence can be found in every living and non-living thing (ducks, trees, rocks and so on) the narrator says okay fair enough but we can find everything else in them too: hate, derision, banality, nihilism, depravity, etc. So there's enough blame for the hell we find ourselves in to go around. No one and nothing is innocent. Or is that the case? The narrator offers the faintest sliver of possibility as the piece comes to its dramatic conclusion.

I did this semi-critique because S{E}AN? said his sketch of me would be worth something one day. I don't know. He didn't get my lips quite right.

-- *Vladimira (Mira) Oblonsky*

from
"the unknowed things"

the unknowed things

So sad to be alive. If it is a question of the interest Archibald drums up it is good to sell. Sad is a vitamin. She asked me: *what happened and where is the she?* I told her I saw the car tire roll slowly over the boy's body and of how I picked him up and of how he smiled at me before I wept. Such [inaudible moaning] is the precursor. In a cul-de-sac many years ago {name unknowed} sat at a table and turned in his chair, lifting his right arm and placing his right hand on his left wrist. He looked to me. This was his milieu. I paused him there and moved him from place to place. In the elevator of my building, when the doors parted he turned in his chair to see the arrival of many people. In the forest outside the city, where I hid behind a tree, he heard the wind and the water and the snapping of branches.

It has been said that the first hand is the dilemma. What to do with it? The second follows according to its nature. The boy fell under the wheel. I moved hand one but hand two did not follow. I pondered the nature of this second hand as I hoped for the collapse of something tangible in me. A collapse of the foundation that kept this worthwhile (by all accounts) structure upright and aware of its own milieu. But there was no collapse even as I took apart what made it recognizable to those who observed.

If a building is the cornerstone of ‘civilization paths’ then Tangier deserves its place in geography. It was a crummy way to start out on the golden trail but I had asked nicely and was rewarded with a catheter to the brain stem. Yesterday nothing drained but today was frisky with no evidence of humanity in the atmosphere. The doctors said I drained an easily quantified amount of--and then a communal huddle followed by ‘well, in any case, everything’s fine’. I reassembled and set my oysters on history.

Everyone knows the plot thickens with the arrival of new invitees. I invited Perry. And then Lily. Likewise Jame. The last ounce of Jame dissolved in my preserves not long after her tale was {action unknowed}. And don’t forget the adventures of the cornbread maker who, despite his Marxist leaning, was always a hero to me. No one knew his real name, though I suspected it was one of those union monikers. The cornbread maker’s second hand always followed accordingly.

We would hope that all futures have but one rule regardless of how those futures originate and that the wisdom of this one rule permeates false theories as well as true theories so the convergence of all that is true and false, although it does not provide the epiphany that would justify a mistaken life, at least makes one pause long enough to realize that the wisdom of this one rule is best and from here onward, there will be a new way.

--Vice Admiral Atsuko Miyazaki, interviewed on the TV2 show 'It's in the Lips'

When the show ended, I wrote a letter in disagreement with the guest's views and harangued the ever-so "quote, unquote" fair host for being a tool of the anti-{cause unknowed} propagandists. To my surprise, I received a response, stating that a vice admiral couldn't be blamed for the consequences of my ingratitude. Such a knowing people, I thought. It was true. Lily had given me everything even when I didn't ask, appearing with unexpected gifts even when I deserved nothing. She told me the most beautiful stories that I, in turn, told to others as if they were my own.

She never said good-bye.

(Or maybe she did and I wasn't listening.)

In the dark end of the forest I see Frau Gretchen's pupae and then her milk situated just so beneath the ever impending palm of shuttle-shoots. We are of a like mind she and I. A minion crawling toward the calm underbrush of snow and the splintered trunk of Tiberius. She said all mornings remain the same. Just above the ground and into a thin forktwist that rebels against the natural movement of the promenade. Drill the {object unknowed} to ferment the dew, an approaching opening, something slender and orb, like the ascendance of a tyrant.

We stood there. Capable of movement but incapable of reason. In the parlance of 'what have we got here?' it was a preamble to a less derisive unknown: sadly, sniff sniff, on this day twenty years ago.

The portly frau misunderstood my discontent and compared it to the time she rolled her eyes at the largest animal enclosure on this side of the peninsula. Up on that hill, during winter, they found a pair of school-girl knickers covered in what could only be described as 'the perfume of the royal stem'.

Certainly, the populace had their druthers. But wiser men believed that such pungency came with a considerably more decisive incision, although it wasn't enough to sever the second hand--the worthless appendage that 1.) hung so proudly and 2.) sought only its advantage. The wives of these wiser men chanted as if in a trance: "hack away at the bits and pieces of all it had done, all the vile, and all the sick". And I confessed to an accomplice that it was a catchy little tune but the strength necessary for such a feat required two arms and the swing of a more foreign musculature.

Lily got down on all fours and asked me to soak in her sunshine. So warm and rubby on the face. A brilliant light that peeked through her whistle. It was a certain kind of paradise if only one could forget where one was.

But it wasn't enough to balm the infected blood, instead injecting more bile into the sting. And yet a bile that tasted like the most succulent honey the amazing honeybee had ever produced. Honey so angelic that it could only be crafted by the god of honey and honey bees. Honey that once coated the befuddled tongue of man made it a morsel that he nibbled on until he was mute and could only buzz-buzz-buzz the words he needed to say: *forgive me for all the wrong that I have done.*

It was a sickly episode. A black canard of an existence that served no purpose if one deed went undone. A puzzle that was none but chaos should one piece not be picked up and put in its proper place. A bird that would not fly should one feather be plucked and not reattached to its swollen dimple. There was time in all of this to make the right move. Frau Gretchen warned me. Jame. Spencer. They collaborated to collect my disjecta and set me on that golden trail. But Lily turned me away and had me roiling in so many timbers until the boy fell upon the ground and lay like peace in the universe.

On a warm night in Tangier, the carpenter falls in love.

I picked up his body and stood before a large window that drew my eyes to a garden where, in time, the existence of many secret villages were discovered: Sangiers and Fingiers, Longiers and Sungiers, pots and kettles, utensils for eating, hat making instruments and unused soles of shoes, moss covered dresses, pliers and balloons, shells of turtles, pictures of owls, indigenous kale, friends.

The boy struggled to smile even as his eyes closed and I wondered why at this most important moment in human history, the sun did not part the clouds and light the most beautiful face that ever veiled the blood of man.

{end unknowed}

a semi-critique of the sun is the monster eye by saskia kang

Thesis: the universe is the mind trying to understand itself.

Almost a decade ago S{E}AN? Gave me an early draft of *The Sun is the Monster Eye*. The word that came to mind then as I read it was "curious". I was curious but most of all I thought the author was curious. Curious about how his own mind worked but also just afraid enough not to ransack through it to cause any permanent damage (as far as I know). Today several words come to mind as I read it. While it's impolite to reduce any work of art to only a few paragraphs much less a few words, I can only say that I felt that I was going through some sort of psychoanalysis while I was reading the story and word association seemed rather appropriate.

The story is about a narrator who wants to meet a dressmaker named Sasha. We're not sure if Sasha makes dresses for others or just herself but we know that she uses a variety of materials. Sasha also had an accident as a child that damaged her pupils and perhaps we are supposed to believe that she makes her dresses without being able to see. It's ambiguous but ambiguity is essential to the story. Is Sasha the ultimate dressmaker who doesn't need eyes to see? Is this symbolism? I've read that this author avoids symbolism in his writing but going back to Plato and even further back symbolism seems to be unavoidable because it's part of how the human mind makes sense of things. Can this story be made sense of? I'm not sure but what I do know is that I felt like tiny little hooks had been attached to my brain and were pulled ever so slightly to give me the sensation that my brain was being stretched and perhaps pulled out of my skull. The ending was implausibly both hopeful and hopeless at the same time. Reading the story didn't make me feel comfortable but it didn't hurt either. Do I understand anything more about the universe than I already understood? Probably not. Or maybe I do and I'm just not aware of it yet. Does the universe understand anything more about itself? I have no idea.

-- *Saskia Kang*

from
"Still Life in Motion"

THE SUN IS THE MONSTER EYE

People think that I am dumb because I haven't had much to say for a long time. But I have been saving up my moments and hiding them behind my 'hello's and 'how are you's. I spoke little and wrote little, instead keeping notes on other people's moments and sometimes speaking of them as if they were my own.

The woman on the phone wants Christmas lights put up around the house before she gets home. She's going to stop by the store and buy those flowers. Those red flowers. I think she called them rhododendrons. She called the person on the other end of the phone James. She drew circles on her note pad while she was talking.

I don't know what to make of other people's moments. I keep thinking that one day I will open my notebook that I've filled with them and find the pages blank. I read them over and over again because they are almost invisible to me and shivery to my touch as if they are hidden behind a thick sheet of ice. But I've collected enough of my own moments now and I feel the urge to relate them. Not for the purpose of having people see them or hear them. I don't really want them to. But my moments are running out of room in here and I don't have anywhere else to put them

Sew dresses Sasha. Don't do anything else.

You'll just have to decide if it's the right thing for you. She said she didn't know. They were quiet for a few blocks. The man's arm brushed against the woman's arm. Twice. Then they walked into an office building.

I finally arrive at Sasha's and I am bursting to tell her something. I knock on her door. I know she is in there but I call to her as if I am not sure. She doesn't mind that I pretend in this way because she says that I pretend in my own way.

It's raining here, but the sun is still visible in the distance. I feel naked in this rain and I feel that the sun is watching me.

I worry now because I wonder if anyone noticed that something fell from my pocket as I was taking my hand out. Flow. Maybe no one (er.) noticed but I have to be more careful. My urges are polarized.

"Sasha."

And then she comes out after a few moments, wearing a dress she has made of squares and flowers, a fusion of geometry and botany and biology. She tells me that her armoire is a circle, and her foot is a square, which is a flower, which is an eyelid that has yet to bloom. She tells me that they are and I believe her. She says that she will show me the proofs very soon.

"Okay", I say.

I tell Sasha okay from time to time because okays are good hiding places. The first step I take implies my long stride and impatience.

"Wait", she says.

She sees how strange the day is. Better than me. She says she sees well because of a child-hood catastrophe (insert insect) that destroyed her pupils (insert tacheon). She says she sees the molecules that make up a circle. She says that all circles are not the same.

"The sun is trying to hide now", she says. "It is hiding a little, but it is still there. And there are so many greens. Yes. So many that I can only see them if I don't think of them."

The pumas are migrating. Sew dresses Sasha.

I remember when Sasha thought a fish was a fish and not a disconnected tongue without fins. She says she knows better now. And yet she says, one day she will know more.

"What are you doing?" she asks me.

I don't know what she is talking about and I think that something has created an impasse between Sasha and myself. Sasha and me. Sasha and I. She asks me what I am doing and I don't know what she is talking about.

But I know the sun is watching. Latitudes display particular motions in congress. And sometimes progress.

"Slow down", she says.

And I do. I've seen others do it.

"Your eyelid is blooming", she says. "Don't you feel it?"

I feel nothing. I can't think of any other words that describe this feeling better.

I'd like to go to the bar and have a glass of whiskey, but Sasha still hasn't moved after our first step. I am a half breed ahead of her and the space between us vibrates the theory of perpendicularity.

Auxiliary note: the theory of perpendicularity states that from any one axis, any point in time (past or future) can be mapped at different degrees along other axes in multiple dimensions. Future points and past points cannot be mapped on the same axis. End.

The vibrations are reaching my nodes. A husband is going away for the weekend.

"Sasha", I say, "can we hurry along?"

I say it normally because I want to have a drink and a cigarette. I want to watch my smoke explode against the bottom of an empty glass.

While I wait for Sasha to catch up, I am propositioned by a vacancy. I enter like someone who--he

Sits in a chair. Maps. Medulla oblongata. Sssssssssssss. Dust.

Sasha has caught up to me now and we continue to the bar. The relative ease of our stroll makes me think about balance and the fundamental flaw that is the essence of bipedism (insert name).

"Sasha", I say.

Sasha's dress is made of circles and flowers and things that I have seen her pick up in different places.

But I had noticed something that will be of help. While I was standing there I saw the same man over and over again. He seems to be walking around the blo(ck) {interesting note on model airplane #3} over and over again. I map a point to a previous past on another axis. I have a secret.

Some pasts are current.

We reach the bar and sit down at a table. I position my head at a forty-five degree angle to the wall beside us.

The circles were not perfectly drawn and some were colored in.

"Sasha", I say, "I am really bursting to tell you something."

"Tell me", she says.

Light travels along a random spine and finds its way into the bar.

"The sun is the monster eye", I say.

I draw circles on a napkin and my eyelid explodes. Petals float to the table. Sasha rubs the side of her glass. At another table someone is looking at us and writes something into a notebook.

Everything stops.

a semi-critique of **when boys sleep** by miranda van amstel

Thesis: put dainty things in dainty boxes

So this was the story that made me want to stop studying and work in a factory. I did for a few months but became bored with factory life and returned to school. I ended up changing my studies from Literature to Structural Engineering. I realized while working in the factory that what I really wanted to do was design boxes. All types of boxes. Boxes for large objects. Boxes for dainty objects. Even boxes for other boxes. I do have a job now designing boxes for dainty objects—objects smaller than the average sized human hand. I think of this story as fitting within one of those small boxes, pushing slightly against the inside, and then unfolding out slowly when the box is opened. Almost shyly—if such an unfolding could take place. But before you opened the box, if you put your ear to it, you would hear the faintest of breaths as if something were using the small amount of air in there. You might ask if this is a dainty story. After all, it fits inside a box designed for dainty objects. But to be fair, it would go too far to call it a story. It would go too far to call it anything for fear of damaging it. It doesn't hold up to the weight of other words. However, if you let it be to use up the little air it arrived with, then it will live for you for a short while before passing into obscurity.

-- *Miranda Van Amstel*

from
"The Unknowed Things"

WHEN BOYS SLEEP

i?

When boys sleep, birds lift their wings to still the branches of trees.

There are events which take place before and after the end. Should a man enter the two spaces formed by these four boundaries he becomes lost for a while. Not very lost. But lost enough to think that he has taken this life for granted. He makes a promise to himself that before the next end, each minute he lives will burst from the amount of life he shall fill it with. He makes this promise secretly—while looking through the window of a bus or standing alone in the corner of an elevator.

He reasons at such moments that he is not very lost, after all, only a little. But in this reasoning germinates the tragedy of being only a *little lost*. He orbits the earth and seeing it *just over there* suffices.

ii?

When boys sleep, the majesty of their dreams are revealed in every drop of rain that falls, in every molecule of air that touches human face, in every cell that glides beneath human skin.

Today the mailbox is empty and I wait for a response. To think about the small room and just outside a forest of blueberries. The white desk. The photo albums and the diary with missing pages.

To think about the short walk to the river. Too long have I suppressed the memories of this life. Of the tree that fell and cleared a path through the clouds. A path to the future.

I make preparations. But in this room, the clouds are darkened by our shadows. Something happens here as Juliet blows the feather from her hand and I watch it float from the window onto the grass. With each turn in its descent, an old room in an old city and the horizon measured by old windmills, the sun three windmills wide and growing, the room five windmills slow as if a ship of long and faithful suffering.

We trace these movements to understand that our happiness is found in the smallest moments of doubt. In the nimble. In the crane on the horizon upon which a boy sits and spies us from the distance. In the faded and opened hand of a woman that can never be drawn again.

iii?

When boys sleep, the universe descends on mankind and for a short while the world trembles with meaning.

Metaphysics, it has been said, is an unwieldy feather and so we must sublimate the chaos of patterns created by the accidental motions of this feather in order to give us an image that approaches that thing for which there is no word.

But this feather is used in many ways. When Juliet moves it along my spine, I think about the room we are in and the window from where I see her bicycle leaning against the tree. When Juliet moves the feather along my spine, I think that I have lived in this room my whole life. With her. Between the soft, white blankets. In the melodies of Chopin. On the wooden floor. In the glass of water on the table through which I see man's caricature of time.

I feel her trace a question mark between my shoulders and we commit to each other's subtle rearrangements in silence. We know we are cursed, if only for a short while, to take our place among the living.

iv?

When boys sleep, the ruminations of future progeny fan our desires.

I sensed from the beginning Juliet's proclivity for distance. I met her by the fountain taking pictures and I moved towards her as if of some other will. In turn she moved and barely so to keep me at bay. I said to her from where I stood *there is a graceful way in which to view the gallows.*

Juliet and I eat at three feet. We sleep at two. We speak at five. So before she speaks she will move away from me. But not now, sitting here on the bed next to me, she draws a secret language on my skin that I will spend my day deciphering. Soon she will leave. Later she will return, leaning her bicycle against the tree, hurrying up the stairs to see me again, her body less of breath that she will encourage me to replace.

v?

When boys sleep, the truth veils itself so we cannot elude it.

The question mark is an ambiguous symbol. At one moment, a representation of deference. At another moment, of defiance. It provokes thought today and leaves the mind immobilized tomorrow. In all objects and gestures. In all faces and events. But at the end of all question marks, one will find a pause. A park bench on which to rest and watch pretty girls take pictures of bicycles and sailboats and of beautiful women talking quietly together by a fountain of horses in which their children play. In this place, such things are possible. The air is finer here. Our lungs more capable.

vi?

When boys sleep, the euphony of silence adorns our every word.

I knocked on the door and Juliet said come in. I sat down beside her on the bed and told her there is something I feel that I cannot put into words. Something about lions and long strands of hair. A pillow and a breeze. She said she felt it too. I took her hand and held it without speaking.

Behind us, the window framed the image of a crane on the horizon, upon which a boy and his sleep created all that was dreamed and not dreamed in this small patch of world that was ours.

vii?

When boys sleep, that which is immutable fragments and finds shelter in the dreams of children.

All one need do is peek through the window. On the crane in the distance, the boy sleeps in the dimly lit night. His face, an image of peace and love. In cities all over the world, known and unknown to you, when the sun sets and his eyes start to close.

In Rotterdam. In Dublin. In Glasgow. In Trondheim. In Bucharest. In Borås. In Helsinki. In St. Petersburg. In Shanghai. In Kyoto. In Lille. In Darfur. In Asmara. In Kuala Lumpur. In Ulan Bator. In Perth. In Bombay. In Lima. In Des Moines. In Alberta. In Juneau. In Skeldon. In Machico. In Barcelona. In Sarajevo. In Washington D.C.

viii?

When boys sleep, all that is beautiful in this world ascends.

Juliet and I ride our bicycle between the rows of mist. Above, a boy the shape of life and what it is to be living curls up and wrenches our plot asunder. A bobwit and allegory of pending trifles, he senses to me her ankle and supple calf, a whittle of such splendor as to make a weighty man no more than an ounce. But there is a strong gust from the horizon and we pound the grind racing, drifting onward into that orbit spoke of but never again, circling the trolley and the carriage and the flat boat on the canal, leaning from the bridge to drink where children play without surrender, a pardon, a sense of grace, turning and turning and turning.

ix?

When boys sleep, all that we have seen and heard and learned is returned to the place of its birth.

Bring out the trotters and me a captive in this room. Their bright regalia and nostrils of flame but fearful of those children who adore them. She (9 hers) pulls love from my mouth and cups it in her hands. We build a tree there and a sailboat of wood, a bicycle for two, a dock from which to leap, and with the flip of a switch, a bright and promising sun. We are afraid to move. While we are here. Closer and closer and closer we stand and in so doing, darken the clouds.

a semi-critique of **drowning maria** by valentino rossi

Thesis: boys and girls fall in love

It is no surprise as I see it for boys and girls to fall in love with people who are wearing clothes of the church. *Drowning Maria* explores this affinity in a majestic way with majestic being something small instead of large. For this the writer is rewarded as if Godot had arrived finally and as someone recognizable to us as an uncle from our childhood. It is not to say that I was moved by the writing but instead to say that I was stilled by it. Even if English is not my first language I somehow understood the writing as rhythm in the sense that music is resistant to the discrimination of our first language and the limitations of our second or third or fourth. But the rhythm was that of a lullaby and not something pressing me to act. It is something sleepy but to sleep in order to get to that state of thinking that is reminding me of a dream.

-- *Valentino Rossi*

from
"the unknowed things"

DROWNING MARIA

When Maria looked out through the tall, open window at the single palm tree on the beach and how the large, flat leaves swayed to the measure of her tapping fingers, she thought back to a time when leaves weren't so friendly to her, when they chased her through the streets of her childhood neighborhood, scraping the concrete violently behind her. Now she was the master of them and tapped her fingers quietly to lull them into sway without alarming them. As a child she longed for winter and snow when the trees were bare and the ground covered so that she might explore the world without anxiety. But in this place she thought it impossible that winter could ever exist again. She would reach out to some distant feeling of ringing bells and the smell of oranges and burning wood but she could never get a hold of it.

In a few weeks she'll return to Chile for her friend's wedding. In a few months she'll ride her bicycle to the apartment of Gaston Ribera for a surprise visit and find him having breakfast with a woman she doesn't know. In a few years, she'll drink coffee at

Mere Juni at the same time every evening and fall in love with the young painter who waits tables and who will change the landscape of art with Piñeroism—a play on his name and the word pin—that will be the start of her unhappiness.

But this morning she tapped her fingers quietly and prefaced the day with a hushed but candid confession to the palm tree about the orgasm she had the night before as she masturbated to the vicar's memory. It was the young vicar's fault she thought for being born so handsome but having become so unattainable. In turn, the night gave birth to a day that felt limitless and opened to her every whim.

She felt as she sat there listening to the ocean that she loved the world again, loved everything and everyone in it, loved humanity with all of its grand and not so grand gestures and foibles, loved the impudence of life in the seemingly endless void that was the universe. And yet, she felt unable to express her feeling in any understandable way.

Go well in this world and may no harm come to you. Be happy. Love. Laugh. Live.

She often thought these things to herself but could never say them to anyone. So she left friends and strangers alike with a smile they might think out of place or an awkward gesture or phrase they shook their heads to once out of her view. What to make of her they thought? What to make of what she said? What to make of the strangely awkward but graceful way she spoke with her hands? Perhaps they thought her naïve, but they'd forget this part of her soon enough as they went on to do things—important things, vital things, serious things, things that mattered—and this part of her would drift anonymously in and out of their lives. Or perhaps they pretended not to recognize this part of her and instead addressed her as if this part of her didn't exist because this part of her always felt out of context to them.

"How are you? Good good. Things are moving. Things are happening. Things. Yes yes. Things I tell you. Things. Moving moving moving. Things are moving."

I met her those few weeks later at her friend's wedding. She sat alone in the church and stared at the fresco on the ceiling. Outside, I spoke to her and asked her if she knew the history of the fresco. She said she didn't so I told her the story of how the great Spanish artist Mirona was commissioned by the governor of the colony to paint memories of home and images of Heaven onto the ceiling of this church. Mirona painted for seven years and when he finished, he unveiled for the governor and colony officials a painting of poverty and suffering, of starvation and cruelty, of torture and deprivation with smiling angels and cherubs interspersed throughout. The governor ordered Mirona to repaint the ceiling or be put to death. Mirona refused. Another artist covered Mirona's fresco with plaster and painted a fresco more to the governor's liking.

But there below the surface of this painting, the other painting still exists.

She seemed genuinely interested and questioned me as to the truthfulness of this tale. I assured her that although she wouldn't find this story in any book that it was entirely true. One need only chip away at those shining images of God and paradise on the ceiling above.

Perhaps when she rode her bicycle to visit Gaston Ribera, she thought back on this story and remembered my face. Remembered how we spoke briefly after a wedding outside an old church and then said goodbye. Maybe when she found Gaston Ribera in his apartment having breakfast with another woman she thought that she could have been with me instead, lying in bed, thinking about how it might be possible to unpaint a fresco in an old Spanish church. But we had said goodbye a long time ago and now she was riding away from his apartment in tears.

But why move ahead? Why let this blissful moment of her watching a single palm tree on the beach sink into the cloudy pool of memory? It would all end soon enough. One day her portrait, painted in the Piñeroistic style, will hang from that very wall behind where she is sitting and watch as she walks into the ocean and disappears.

a semi-critique of **Love Letters from Satan** by Paul Eugene Paul

Thesis: don't forget your tummy

Forgetfulness provided the benefit of Satan always being able to see the world with wonder. So for us (the readers) Satan always seems to have a certain innocence about him.

From the letters we know that Satan had other feelings, but hope was his favorite. Hope made him think that he might be interesting and capable. There was a whole world spinning above him. A world where interesting and capable people debated the characteristics of his soul or the enigmatic and barely graspable origins of his consciousness. He was desperate to be a part of those conversations but believed that his desperation would leave him at a desperate loss for words.

The letters also make it clear that he felt slightly conspiratorial about the thought that he was neither interesting nor capable because “He” had said that as a child Satan was bursting with both qualities. The “He” pretended things with him that Satan believed would one day be true—that he was a special child and that he had an intangible quality that would sparkle under the right circumstances. It was the more noble part of that sometimes awkward entanglement between adult and child that engenders encouragement or humiliation. Certainly, a close reading of the letters will show that Satan was encouraged. But they also suggest that his human body and all that it was already filled with—extraneous of any encouragement or humiliation—went its own way.

Note: Lilibeth Spato reminds me of Fever, the girl who works at the bookstore not far from me. I've spoken to Fever a few times but never had a real conversation with her unless quoting passages from the books I borrow from the bookstore count as conversation. The first time I spoke to her I said: *logic is doubtless unshakeable but it cannot withstand a man who wants to go on living*. To which she replied: *doubtless*. Strange huh?

-- *Paul Eugene Paul*

from
"The Unknowed Things"

Love Letters from Satan (Letter 1)

Letter 1

Dear Friend,

It would have better for me if I had been a dairy farmer instead of Satan but my selflessness was ingrained in me at an early age. How could I allow another to suffer the humiliation and ostracism I have suffered? You might think it difficult for me to find a pleasant little nook to settle into but I have found a small room to live in above a tobacco shop across from the University Hospital where I was born Tundey Abikinaba. You would be surprised to know that despite my lack of formal education or military training I still manage to pay the two-hundred and fifty dollars rent each month, which conveniently enough, includes all the washing of my dirty linens and a once a month shining of the old boots worn by my father.

I apologize I could not meet with you last week but I did hear the news that Roger Spato insulted you while at the theatre. Don't worry my friend. I assure you that I am Roger Spato. I am also Spato's wife Penelope and Lilibeth, their darling daughter. I write letters to her of a startling clarity. I can send a copy of one to you if you like for I make copies of all my letters, including this one. It is, with all humility, an endeavor of a historical nature.

I write to tell you I bring the world a new way. Or rather a new perspective of an old and calamitous philosophy. By the way, if while reading this letter you happen to hear music, do not be surprised. Twice a week, a quartet plays outside my window and they arrive punctually and in tune. At the moment, they are applying themselves to a vivacious adaptation of a Janacek concerto.

Speaking of music, dear friend, the grocery store is not far and I would like to invite you for a little bite of supper one of these good nights. I am on very good footing with the grocers and I doubly assure you that they put aside all the best legumes for me. Is it not bizarre how France, Germany, and England are claimed to be the fashionable legume countries now when everyone knows the best legumes are to be found here? Imagine my surprise when I picked up the newspaper this morning to read of this. It is such a tedious endeavor to appease the Europeans but appease them I will. Only in the French language is it even possible to subscribe to such flighty notions so I will assume they were the ring leaders of this malfeasance.

As to our supper and my explanation of the new way, I urge you to accept my generous invitation. We are both free men, unencumbered by career or family concerns and one night away from all the mind-numbing festivities of this time of year might do you well. Do not be troubled that only I will be talking. You will certainly have events to relate to me as it pertains to the new opera I am writing. You did hear did you not? A liberating account of the dog races played out on a bifurcated stage where the upper half represents--what else?--heaven, and the lower half, my little room. Wear panties. The new way is rather warm.

Love always,
Satan

a semi-critique of **beth v. beth singular** by Thor Ruiz

Thesis: there are no characters except those drawn by hand

The story is a tale of two people and lays bare for us the tension between inflection and innuendo (as the poet says) and encourages us to posit on the absence of what makes each what they are.

For Beth, who one finds but is never there, the crowd is invisible. No matter how distracted or preoccupied or late we are in looking when at last we look our eyes fall immediately upon her and no one else. At the most obscure angles and bend of our neck we find her. In the most uneasy and unexpected circumstances we find her. She is never beside us before we find her and then we wait or meet her halfway and while we are waiting or meeting her halfway we feel the breeze on our face and we are overcome by a feeling of happiness.

For Beth Singular who is always there before we ever find her, the crowd is never small enough. If she were to walk hand in hand with just one other human being along a path framed by (let us say) pear trees on either side she would be obscured by the shade of a single leaf. We think we see her but—refocusing—we see that it is not her. It is the shadow of a passing sparrow or the single loose strand of someone's tightly clasped hair (and we wonder if it is hers). We lament that we cannot find her like we find Beth. We endeavor and while we endeavor she is suddenly there beside us. We never see her before she is there. And when she is there we feel the breeze on our face and we are overcome by a feeling of happiness.

And so we ponder the very real possibility of not finding Beth or of Beth Singular not being there. We are filled with dread. We don't understand the configurations of a life that brought us to this—the entanglement of the relationship we have with each. We cannot make sense of why this is so and we worry that to delve too far into either would be to shake loose the tightly woven but delicate threads that bring them to us in their own way. We think that one day we will understand. Not because we are thoughtful or inspired but because the reason will simply become clear to us.

--Thor Ruiz

from
"The Unknowed Things"

beth v. beth singular

Beth Susan has hyper-extended lymph nodes.

In the evenings she cooks or bakes. Never both. Sometimes she glazes a turkey before she puts it in the oven. There's no need to tell the story of her life because it can be summed up in this way: she is an ordinary person of ordinary ability. If one were to search for any magic in her routine, one would curse her existence. We could say she had choices. Instead of going here she might have gone there. Instead of doing this she might have done that. But if we curse her let us remember that she is not entirely to blame. At a young age she was set on a certain path and she continued along that path knowing nothing more.

And yet let us suppose she did know more. Let us suppose that at the age of twelve she saw a picture of Mongolian horses and later that night dreamed of palm trees. Perhaps…but really, what good would it have done? The courage to take a false step was not in her.

We'll say remember but it's not always about memory. The first virgin of civilization swept the streets outside her hut. There were the Francophiles and the Anglophiles but none restored order to the universe. So memory doesn't always hold sway. Doesn't reach out. Doesn't get Beth Susan wet. The most we can do for her is to glorify the ordinary. To say, for example, that the sun reaches her kitchen floor from a window through which she sees the grass and the overhanging branches of a nearby tree.

In time she became a precedent. A figure of imaginable awe. And then a subterranean falter of paprika and marmalade as she brought the curtain to the porch and spread it on the floor, searching for the circles and swelled-Friday in a singular expression of darker turning. Sensitive (sensitive) girl.

I knocked at a noble hour and upon being invited in said: "Good morning Beth Susan".

The day before, on a Sunday, pommes frijoles were served by the carpenter who designated the house and specifically the bedroom, the bed, and Beth Susan as things and person to think of while shuddering.

"Good morning", she said.

I sat for a coffee and remarked casually as to the paint peeling on the outside of her door. A sad summary for such a golden block or not quite, but close. She stared.

It is remarkable Beth Susan, your lumps are figuratively to die for and may I without regret continue my sympathy and curiosity for the sake of conversation. Laud me but make no mention of what is base as some poet might say for the sake (again) of sounding profound. But I have dreamed of you as if on a boat on a still, black sea. And the night. And the stars. How to make mention of them as they are? But may I, as I have always wanted, be the first to say that your sorrow is mine. It is mine and I come to take it from you.

Languid night. Three pence fold (comes the stolid).

The mollification of her stamina, free but not without its proclivities, proved a disaster to the carpenter, who hammered immorally throughout the house. Lest she forget the importance of shingles and their proper nailing I casually suggested an inspection of their aft and foreaft.

"Have you felt a--what shall I call it? A transition in your ear?"

She responded to the contrary but did confess, albeit reluctantly, of a colorless blur. The garments, the placards, the restive clink. I sensed her desire to keep them hidden. But what of the curtain Beth Susan? Is it not a child of the tropics? Relate this to me and in such a way as to approve of blood.

The Mongolian horses etc., etc… The palm trees, etc., etc…

So she's not the girl sitting on the couch. Her walls aren't blue. She doesn't have a ponytail or wear old shoes that have become fashionable.

Beth Susan, let me take your sorrow. It belongs to me. We are but two creatures you and I, an irrelevant species, hard pressed to die without a feeling of relief. The last feeling. The truest feeling.

Etc., etc...

a semi-critique of **interior without violin case** by orble

Thesis: the last of its kind to be born sometimes dies young and is forgotten

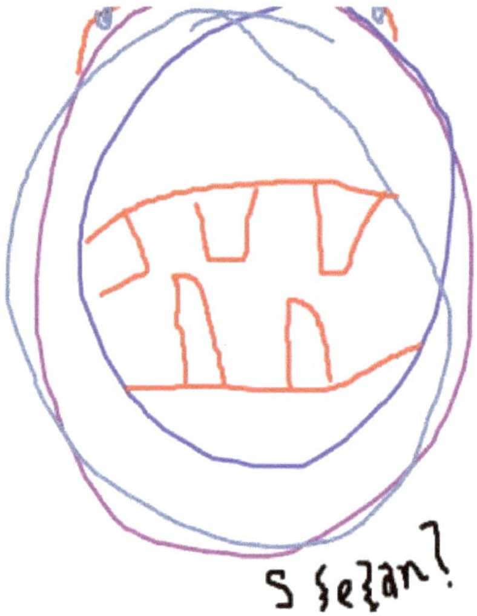

In this tale S{E}AN? writes of a pylon maker whose hobby is following people around. This was the story that inspired me to talk about the weather. For example, today there's a low pressure system building to our south that's being pushed towards us by warm ocean air. There's also a high pressure system coming from the north and if the two meet there could be storms. But it's raining right now and it's going to be a grey, drizzly day, so don't forget those umbrellas.

--orble

from
"Still Life in Motion"

interior without violin case

somewhere in this room, i am dying

I think it is dawn because the sky outside the window is a lighter shade of dark blue and the buildings are blue with distinct black outlines. There is a bridge that has stairs, but I can't see that there is no water beneath it. The walls in here are dark save for a painting that hangs off canvas and a few squares of canvas that hang unfinished above my bed.

the chair

The chair is woven in a traditional pattern. The contoured slats are reminiscent of the early 19th century. If I had another chair, I might place it beside the chair I have to make a love seat. Or I might place them facing each other in case two people wanted to have a conversation. Or I might place them back-to-back if two people didn't want to have a conversation. I once thought of such things. I would have liked another chair, but I couldn't afford one. I'm supposed to have two chairs in my room. Dying in my chair, I wouldn't be uncomfortable, but I've placed a canvas that I'm painting on it and my painting would be destroyed. There is no violin case on my chair.

the bamboo rug on the floor

I didn't consider the rug much. I didn't think about how it would look where I would lay it. I knew that not many people would walk on it because barely one person could fit in this room. I remember thinking that I wanted something neutral to place beneath a chair that I would use as an easel to place canvasses on. Wool is rich. Nylon takes on different personalities and dyes well. But I have a bamboo rug. When it rains and I forget to close my window my bamboo rug gets wet. I try not to spill paint on my rug. My rug anchors the open space in my room, which isn't very large. Part of my chair and most of my footrest, which is a plastic crate that I've painted light brown to match my chair, and which I use to sit on when I paint, rest on my bamboo rug. There isn't much room to stretch my body on the bamboo rug.

the curtain hanging on the window

I'd like to tell you that my curtain adds color and texture to my room, but it doesn't. It's a yellowish-brown color without any patterns. Sometimes I don't want people looking into my room, even though I live on the fourth floor but think I should live on the second floor. I can cover my window with the curtain. I've thought about blinds or shades, but then I wouldn't get enough light in and I need to have enough light to make part of the wall a little lighter than the rest of the wall. The curtain hangs down to the floor. I don't know what would happen if I was dying on the floor with my back against the curtain. I would probably knock over the table that sits in front of my window. Maybe I would pull the curtain as I fell over one last time. Maybe the fallen curtain would cover my body.

beneath the clock

Clocks are something people are always looking at. For this reason, I don't have a clock in my room.

on the floor beside the bed

One of the reasons I live here is because of the floor. It took me years to find a room with this type of floor. I think it is unstained wood, very dark brown, laid in a herringbone pattern. I imagine it to be Brazilian or Spanish. I've covered part of the floor with the bamboo rug, but the floor can still be seen and walked on along the window and beside my bed. If it were not for what I see outside my window, the floor would be my favorite part of this room. Still, I might be somewhat obscured by the chair and footrest that sit partially on the bamboo rug. If I'm bleeding and I'm not sure that I am, I wouldn't want my blood to go missing in the creases of such a dark place. My body would cover most of the floor beside the bed and also hide part of the red blanket with white flowers.

the table by the window

The table is an antique table with four legs. I'd like to say it is all white, but the legs are really a bluish gray and the top of the table is yellow. I usually have a tray there with a glass of water on it. I think I still do. Or I should. The table is tall and graceful and rises to the height of half the window, which is large and starts only a foot or so from the floor. The surface of the table has become distressed by time. There would be no space beneath such a thing to languish.

the bed against the wall beneath three unfinished paintings

The bed frame is made of flimsy wood that has been surprisingly easy to care for and the blanket is red with white flowers, which are not flowers but white circles. Nobody would know if I were losing blood on this blanket, unless the white flowers turned red. Sometimes I think the bed is leaning because when I lie on it I feel like I am sitting on a chair on an abandoned veranda that leans over a bustling street. Streets bustle, especially along the quay of Saint-Michel. The bed is where there isn't a naked woman resting on her side with her hands behind her head. That is where I should be dying. But I don't know.

a semi-critique of **diary of a composer: a one note symphony** by Carmen Mérimée

Thesis: the sun, the sun, the sun...

To know me is to know music and the bridge to heaven. In all the world and its history the mechanism through which one forgets (for bursts) the isolation and (out of fear of misshapen cartography) immolation of the self (everyone has their own and mine is self).

I understand this symphony as a woman in a lace dress, her earrings the Romanian gymnast. We make her so and her soul in paradise. The symphony comes from her tears. The cartography of her hip and spine when she turns—they come from her tears. The harmonica written on her smooth belly in backward arcs around her naval a spiral and aloft we spy (as such aloft) the outlines of her remarkable, unconquered lands.

She cannot hate us no matter the depths of our cruelty. She wants to do something (if just for a moment). Something to the world (if just for a moment). She is more noble than we (we hear it in the singular note). She falls apart whole. She comes to pieces whole. And we are to blame.

-- *Carmen Mérimée*

from
"One Note Symphonies"

diary of a composer: a one note symphony

blue balloon

Malene rests on her back with her right leg pointing toward the wooden ceiling. A blue balloon descends on her from a hanging stained-glass lamp, and she raises her right arm, then spreads her fingers to push it gently away. She glances at you and turns onto her side.

Your eyes move casually from her breasts to the book you are reading, and the blue balloon waits for her to roll onto her back again before falling towards her face.

The first novels you read to her were westerns, during which time she wore cowboy hats and boots, and once even a full Indian headdress. Then you tiptoed on to romances, but skipped the details of seduction, leaping over paragraphs with a simple "they went into the bedroom and closed the door." You were terrified.

It was only recently that you stumbled upon the courage to read the more amorous, even erotic narrative, and began adding details, lengthening sentences to a few paragraphs, and paragraphs to a few pages, with the result lying comfortably naked before you.

You cross your legs (thin pants) to hide your growing erection, and continue reading where you left off.

diary of a composer

...I whispered 'hello' into my cigarette and exhaled, guiding the smoke towards a woman sitting at one of the front tables. But my message reached a man only two tables away who turned and smiled.

"Not you," I said, shaking my head.

The man sneered and looked away. The band was taking the stage when I took my trumpet from its case, stood on my chair and played one note, holding it for as long as I could. People glared at me in amazement. Napkins were beginning to rise from the tables, but I was interrupted by two waiters who stomped toward me.

I jumped down from the chair, took a quick bow for my appreciative audience, and left the small café, my trumpet's one note (h flat) still buzzing in my ears.

You see music lover, I have spent my whole life composing a symphony, and have written one note, one perfect note...

a dolphin passing

...the Palae Bar on Ny Adelgade was filled with people. Outside, animals crowded the windows: dogs, cats, birds of every kind. Someone screamed (jerking his hand back and forth like a woodpecker) he saw a dolphin pass by, but no one turned to look--Cæcilie was singing.

'...no time for chittin' and chattin' and chittin'...'

(cue piano solo)

The dolphin was me, and it is peculiar that someone mistook me for a dolphin, because there really is no resemblance (other than the glossy, wet look of my skin). I don't like swimming, unless the water is deep--ocean deep, and even then it's only the sensation of floating from bottom to top that I relish. The act of swimming itself never appealed to me. (In fact, between you and me, I don't know how to swim, and have never been near an ocean my entire life)...

(piano fades, cue drum solo)

a flying rook

...the dull brass of my trumpet reflects a rising sun in my opening and closing eyes. I have a frightening secret to tell you music lover, prepare yourself.

(drum roll, the sound of thunder)

It is I who make the sun rise, and if I so desire, can make it stay fixed in the sky for as long as I play my symphony. Modestly stated, I am the most dangerous human being in the world, for I fear (with practice) that I could make the sun rise so high it would disappear; its rays wouldn't reach the Earth and everything would be in darkness.

An old man in a nearby balcony appears moments after me and I free one hand from my trumpet to wave to him, but he doesn't wave back. It is the same every morning.

After raising the sun, I walk to Amagertorv and play my symphony over and over again until darkness falls. Three drunks throw bottle caps in my hat; others toss me a few kroner. I'll admit it is a meager amount, but I don't leave discouraged (what is money to me?). Throughout the day I feel the wind picking up, and witness with my own eyes, hats flying from heads, and a chess piece (a rook I believe) rising towards a broken tree limb...

a torn page

You glance over the books on the shelf in search of a novel that will help you take the next step with Malene, and you finger de Sade's Juliet, but move on. (A well-planned step remember, not a reckless leap.)

Your eyes work backward to P, Paya, Señor Oneypa Paya, and you pull out the master's latest work (Don Quixote's Map of the World), an erotic expedition of the female body. You browse through a few pages when you notice a piece of paper trapped between the books and the shelf. You see what's written on the paper and gasp (actually gasp) in amazement.

"What does it say?"

You don't answer, but look to see if anyone is watching you, then hide the paper under your jacket. You flip conspicuously through Paya's novel, replace it on the shelf, and leave the bookstore.

windmills

If Don Quixote were to mount his pitiable steed Rocinante and go in search of adventure today, he would be arrested for trespassing. His map of the world has changed from vast spaces and open fields to the naked body of a woman--a frontier as ambiguous and complex as Don Quixote's.

But I can't believe that you, faithful reader, are still searching for adventure. Together, you and Malene have visited Dodge City, Paris, St. Petersburg. You have fought bandits, married, divorced, bore children, honeymooned in Singapore, had affairs, grew old, and even died together. But when Malene smiles, you wonder if it is a smile at all; if her hand caressing the sofa is a flirtatious intimation of things to come between you or just capricious housework? Are those giants or windmills off in the distance?

(Speak philosopher…)

It isn't adventure you're searching for dear reader, but certainty. The certainty of a smooth, heavy stone in your hand, or of a dense book. You can be certain of those things. You feel their weight. But you can't be certain about a strand of a woman's hair, or of a woman's love. Such things lack the weight of certainty. They float away, vanishing like words read from a page, specters of an already grasping memory.

I have come to the conclusion that you aren't acting like a man at all (vacillating, rationalizing, procrastinating). You aren't like the characters in the novels you read to Malene, and don't dare attempt an assault on those delicate borders I have established between you two.

However, we grant you some reprieve, for you were last seen (good eyes Sancho) mounting a horse, grumbling in a voice that was hardly your own, about giants somewhere in the distance.

unmeasured sky

...I am on a ferry crossing the sound to Malmö. The sun beams down on me. Earlier this morning, for the first time in my life, I woke up late. I thought of the confused, certainly terrified people in the world who expected sunlight already. But when I rushed out onto my balcony, I realized the sun was making a rapid ascent without me.

It was I who became confused.

I couldn't believe my symphony was being performed without me. Yet, before my disbelieving eyes, a red-orange note scaled a barless, unmeasured sky.

I gave my trumpet a suspicious sidelong glance to which it responded with a sinister gleam. (I had sensed in the last year or so a growing ambition in the devious horn.)

I grasped the situation immediately and struggled to hide my feeling of panic, smoking a cigarette, walking around the room, speaking as if to remind myself of plans made for the rest of the day.

Then, like a sudden fortissimo, I charged the unsuspecting instrument and locked it in its case. I decided to get rid of it, but quickly, before the sun disappeared forever. I went to a pawnshop and traded in my hat for another trumpet.

Don't worry music lover, I am the near antonym of stupid. I realize just as you have (you have realized it haven't you?) that if I simply throw the trumpet overboard, it will make itself float to the surface. Even sealed as it is now, it still raises the sun higher and higher.

I will take the twisted brass into the sound myself and anchor it somewhere deep, where its diabolical rendering of my symphony will be muffled forever. Then I will play my h flat symphony on my new trumpet and float safely back onto the ship. Tomorrow I will raise the sun as always, wave to the old man, then walk to Amagertorv.

But before I go music lover, I must confess that for a brief moment this morning, hidden in the shadows of panic and fear, a feeling of relief gripped me. The sunrise is a great responsibility...

the heaviness of love makes blue balloons float

You dismount and walk into the room where for the last year or so you have read to Malene. She sits naked on the couch, playing with the blue balloon,

and you sit beside her. She is startled.

"Isn't he going to read to me?" she asks.

"I don't know," I reply.

"Yes," you say.

You look down at the solitary piece of paper you found at the bookstore and lean over to Malene,

singing into her ear.

"Again," she says breathlessly.

You take a deep breath, and once more sing into her ear (this time the left one).

Malene puts her arms around you and pulls you on top of her as she kicks the blue balloon away and watches it float outside the window. You relish the heaviness of your own body lying on top of hers as you tear the page into pieces (pieces I try in vain to collect), humming over and over again, softer each time, into her ear.

Malene brushes some lint from the sofa's arm with her free hand. (revenge of a jealous author)

the old man waves

...you didn't think you would hear from me again, did you music lover? But here I am, and here is what happened--*sans drame ou melodrame*.

I forced the treacherous instrument under a large rock near swaying kelp, then put the new one to my lips. I closed my eyes and played my symphony, holding it longer than I had ever held it before, and felt a rush of water and air surrounding my body.

When I opened my eyes, I saw København below me. Around me, there were fish, hats, picnic benches, people, bicycles, people on bicycles, circling passing clouds.

A blue balloon drifted to and fro and I grabbed it by its string (I have it in my hand even now). I saw the old man with his feet pointing toward the sky, clutching the railing of his balcony with both hands, and I waved to him. He released one hand to wave back, and the other hand slipped and he floated away.

My tears float as well music lover, because I am sad to tell you that my diary has come loose in this wind, and the pages fly about like leaves. I must find them, because my symphony (my life's work!) is written there, and strange as it may seem, it has--*absolument*--vanished from my memory...

Part 5

S{E}AN? REAPPEARS

i

It was later in the day that I found out about Deaf. After the plate of eggs and the personification of grace. I thought about Cicero and Seneca for no other reason than he had spoken of them. I didn't know what Deaf's last words were. Maybe "why". Maybe "what".

Fever understood how I carried my suffering. It was an important part of any relationship. I suffered without *ordeal*, without expression. I knew she wanted to share my suffering but she knew that she couldn't. At least not when she wanted to. My suffering was mine to do with as I pleased. One day I might share it. But when and where I didn't know.

In any case, there were still things to do. Still showers to take and teeth to brush and food to cook and shoes to tie and bicycles to park. Most things didn't take on any greater meaning than they did before.

I sat under the tree in the backyard and looked at the word "amputake" still scrawled on the house. I thought about the missing boy and wondered what he had been doing all that time he was missing. I closed one eye and looked around. The world still looked the same to me but I didn't like seeing it that way.

ii

People still talked to me—people who didn't know about what happened to Deaf. Just like people might have talked to the parents of the missing boy. I wasn't comparing the two. A boy was a child. But how to answer questions about what I thought about a football match or where I wanted to go for lunch? I thought nothing. Was I a fucking creep now? Maybe I was just staring into a vortex of misery and not some woman's décolletage. Did she think about that? Even death didn't erase the memory for me. What good was it?

Fever came over and put her arm around me. I thought she had gotten over the neighborhood watch meeting incident. I didn't know what happened. Maybe it was the booze. At the time it felt right but looking back on it I suppose it only felt a little right. Not as right as it did that night. I thought that as the days went by it would feel less and less right until one day some time into the distant future it would feel perfectly right.

"The police came by yesterday" she said.

I shrugged my shoulders.

"It was about Deaf", she said.

"Deaf? Not about the boy?" I asked.

“Well, the boy’s back isn’t he?”

“Yeah but why are they asking about Deaf? What did they want?” I asked.

“Nothing really. Just wondering if we knew what might have happened to him.”

I knew what happened to Deaf. What I didn’t know was how to talk about it or how to feel about it. When I was a child I had feelings for long periods of time. If I was happy I felt happy for a long time. If I was sad I felt sad for a long time. But when I got older I was only happy for a few minutes. And then I was sad. I was angry the next minute. I was hopeful a minute later. All my feelings wanted me at the same time. They pulled me in different directions and I could never be sure of what I was feeling about anything. I couldn’t separate them. I felt everything at once.

iii

On my way to the neighborhood watch meeting I saw that the sign outside Café Hopeless had changed. When I arrived with Deaf the sign read “Pears”. But as I walked away alone I saw that it read “Apophenia”.

(apophenia – making the unrelated seem connected)

Deaf decided that he didn’t want to go to the neighborhood watch meeting, after all. We had one vodka shot too many and he didn't like neighbors. On principle, I didn't like neighbors either but there really was no reason not to like neighbors. They usually left me alone. But we didn't have the same interests (how would I know?). I didn't want to hear about juicing or roads or streetlamps (if that's what they talked about). I didn't care. Fuck all of that.

I needed to pee but I had practiced for moments like this and if I didn't hurry I would miss the meeting and Fever would be upset. I didn't want to upset Fever. I loved her. And who knows? Maybe on my way to the neighborhood watch meeting I'd see the missing boy walking down the street and drag him to the meeting with me and tell everybody that we didn't need to meet, after all—save your concern for your curtains. I'd just drop him in the middle of the floor like I would drop a tennis ball. He'd bounce until he ended up rolling into a corner somewhere and we'd all stare at him once he stopped moving. I told Deaf that if the meeting ended early I'd go back to the bar. He said he'd be there.

iv

I remember when the police came to the house the day after the boy disappeared. I saw television cameras outside. I thought that one of the reporters would eventually stop me on the street and ask me questions about what I knew but none of them ever did. I imagined saying nice things about the boy and his family—of how I saw them outside playing together (like a happy family) or riding their bikes while the grandfather sat in a chair and watched. And that got me to thinking about what people who were stopped on the street by reporters would say about me. They could probably only muster that I was quiet and that they could never imagine I did this or that or that this or that happened to me.

I didn't know anything about other people either. I would probably say the same thing. I told Fever that we needed to learn one or two interesting facts about the people who lived around us so that if we were ever stopped on the street and asked about them, we would have something more interesting or meaningful to say than everybody else. She said she already knew some interesting facts. The people across the street had a blind dog. The two boys behind us were adopted twins. And the people who lived next to us weren't married. I didn't say anything to her because I couldn't figure out if those were interesting facts or not. But I trusted Fever and if she thought those were interesting facts then there was a good chance that they were.

v

All the neighbors were at the neighborhood watch meeting (Burton, Mira, Saskia, Miranda, Valentino, Paul, Thor, Carmen, and Orble). It was like a missing boy's fan club. I saw their names written on a piece of paper that I had to sign to memorialize my presence. But I left the next line blank and added my name beside Fever's where it belonged. Secretly I wanted the paper destroyed. If this was to become an historical document of some importance I wanted to be excluded. That's really all I could think about while they were blabbing.

Where's the boy? Where could he be? What do you think happened to him? It's sad. A shame. The streetlamp by our house is out. Maybe that had something to do with it. If my curtains were a little more sheer I might have seen what was going on outside. Where's the boy?

"I want that piece of paper destroyed!" I yelled. "Des-fucking-troyed!"

Fever looked at me. She tried to hush me by shaking her head. But I was beyond a hush. I stood up and kicked my chair backwards. I thrust my arm forward.

"Give me that fucking piece of paper!" I pointed.

I lifted the table over with my left hand and moved towards the object of my growing annoyance. But on my way there I felt an urge to pee. I was stopped in my tracks. I turned around, quickly unzipped my zipper, and started to pee all over the floor. Despite all my months of practice I couldn't hold it when it mattered most. I thought for sure everyone would notice since they had already been looking at me. But they were startled by the arrival of a boy and girl who walked through the door and stood in front of them. I caught Fever's eye. I thought she would be angry but I saw the slightest smile on her face—barely perceptible unless you knew Fever. I looked over my shoulder and saw that the boy and girl were each holding a book.

The neighbors stood up and surrounded the boy. Could it be? Or was I still drunk? Was it him? Why hadn't I seen him on my way to the meeting? If I had plucked him from the street then this meeting would have turned out differently. Maybe he heard about the meeting and decided to show up. I finished peeing, pulled up my zipper, and turned around to look at them. Yes it was him. The little fucker had returned with a girl in tow. And for one reason or another I felt relieved.

vi

Deaf's last words to me when I left the bar were not his own. He said: "You know what Marlowe said: *the stars move still, time runs, the clock will strike*."

He timed it perfectly as I opened the door to leave (as he always did). But I didn't know what Marlowe said. All I knew was that Deaf said he'd be there when I returned. But I never returned. I went home after the neighborhood watch meeting and fell asleep. A few weeks after the funeral, I returned to Café Hopeless and saw the bartender.

"Hi," I said. "I'm Deaf's friend."

"I know," she said.

I didn't know what to say but I felt connected to her through Deaf. She stopped in at the funeral dressed in her work clothes. She wasn't the only one I felt connected to Deaf through but she seemed like a new connection that no one else knew about so it felt like a secret connection and secret connections were sought after around the world. I had also started to read about nihilism since Deaf died. So I could have a conversation with her about nothing. I wasn't trying to replace Deaf. I was just trying to remember him and help her remember him. But I didn't know how to start a conversation with her.

"Deaf's dead."

"To thine own fucking self be true."

"It's good to be alive."

Sometimes there is an understanding of the world and everyone's place in it at the very moment that you're trying to understand it. It pulls you in. Bends all things towards itself. But never enough before it's gone and the world is the world again. I didn't say anything to the bartender. I had my drink and moved on.

vii

On my way to the tennis court I saw the boy riding his bicycle. He was back and I suppose everything had returned to normal, although I saw his mother looking out the window of their house.

And for no particular reason I wanted her to feel what I was feeling—a strong desire to hurt people who hurt people. I knew in the deepest part of me that was human that I wanted to punish those who were evil and that I would take pleasure (a lot of pleasure) in it. Not a normal, modern kind of pleasure—a more satisfying, primal pleasure. I wanted to become the people I hated most because I couldn't hurt them as myself. I had to be like them. And then I had to be myself again. But I didn't know what happened to the boy. Maybe he ran away to a shoe factory to find some shoes. I was only using him because sometimes the idea of being a monster felt good.

Vladimir was already on the court waiting for me, swinging his racquet back and forth. In half an hour I would be gasping for breath and collapse into a sitting position. So different from how I felt when I arrived. This would be my last death.

viii

If it were possible I would have compared my death to Deaf's death. Deaf stumbled as he walked away from the café, tried to gather himself, but lurched forward, then sideways, and trying to regain his balance, fell and hit the side of his head against the concrete. The bartender said there was nothing for him to trip on (she was waving goodbye to him). She ran over to his motionless body but he had already died in the short distance. She told police that he had been drinking but I'd seen Deaf walk drunk many times. I'd seen him run drunk. I'd seen him dance drunk. They always want to say it's the bad thing that kills people. Because they think death is bad. But sometimes it's the good thing that kills people.

Deaf may have tripped over something no one else could see. Maybe he turned around to look at the bartender while he was walking because he liked her and he could see that she liked him—such a small, barely perceptible thing. Almost invisible to people who weren't paying attention.

Was this Deaf's last death? I didn't know. I only knew that death was heart-breaking and I didn't understand how it was possible to survive it. As for myself, I wanted to see the world in ten thousand years. In five thousand years. In five hundred years. In fifty years. Maybe it was asking too much to live in it but I just wanted to catch a glimpse of what it would look like when I was no longer around.

My last death was balanced. Balance was important in life. If I had died alone someone would have found me in a position that was perfectly in order with the universe.

ix

Fever came outside and told me that she wanted to move. I was sitting on the curb by the road. I hadn't thought about moving but she was right. Fever was right about a lot of things. I didn't like the tiles in our kitchen, after all. And the carpet had started to fray. It was ugly. She was right about that too. It was no longer enough to find beauty in beautiful things. Ugly things had to be beautiful too. And anything that wasn't beautiful was useless. It all started to fucking bother me and push through my brain like weeds in my *planned-but-not-yet executed* garden.

"Where do you want to go?" I asked her.

She sat down next to me. She wasn't wearing shoes and I worried she might step on something sharp when we walked back into the house.

"We'll find some place," she said. "Maybe to an open field during summer where we can see trees in the distance and birds flying above us in a clear sky with soft-looking white clouds and beyond that the sea where our walks end by rocks that waves lightly crash upon. Until evening. Until we sleep—our eyes closing as slowly as the sun descending behind the horizon."

I leaned closer to Fever so that my shoulder was touching hers and thought about Aristophanes and the dilemma Dionysus faced when choosing between Euripides and Aeschylus and I couldn't help but marvel at the Greeks and their handling of the disorienting effects of nihilism.

But one day our eyes will close. One day we'll become quiet and our struggle will be over. The wind will blow over us. Birds will watch us from the trees. In the forest, cats will paw at the moist decay of nature. And above us, far above us, farther still, and even farther, the universe will remain unchanged.

The boy rode by us on his bicycle and waved as if he had never been missing. Fever waved back to him but my heart was flint.

x

Of all the sports, tennis is the only one in which you know how free you are with another person. Was your shoulder loose? Did your wrist snap? Did your arm fly? Any sense of tightness was a reflection of the hierarchy of the relationship you had with the person across the net. So when I played tennis for the first time with Fever I knew. I thought that some people probably wondered why she was with me.

Fever was the kind of woman even the most impolite men held the door for. I would see them slow down to pretend like they were looking for something in their pockets and then at the perfect moment act surprised that she was behind them and then (as every single one of them always did—except for me on the day I met her), reach their arm out, pull the door open, and watch her walk through before following closely behind her to get another glimpse of the outline of her jaw behind her hair or occupy the space she had just left.

I, on the other hand, was a man women didn't hold the elevator for (a "fucking creep") even if they saw me coming. They'd pretend like they didn't see me. And that was okay with me. I had gotten used to women not holding the elevator for me. But Fever did. She held the elevator for me. It's a strange world.

--END--

On Symbolism In Jenufa

Still Life in Motion

The story *I Think Her Name Was Alice* started with a working title of *I Think Her Name Was Albert* in order to hide Alice's true identity. The title was later changed when someone suggested that S{E}AN? write a story about Alice. But it wasn't immediately changed to the famous title it has now. Titles in draft versions included: *Gray Alice, Alice, Fucking Alice, and RoboAlice, Why Waitresses Look Weird.* Those titles were already taken, however, and S{E}AN? simply replaced Albert with Alice in the original title

~~Parts of the brain that lobbied for a cameo in *The Sun is the Monster Eye* included the cerebrum, the parietal lobe, and the thalamus. The cameo eventually went to the medulla oblongata which popped into S{E}AN?'s brain without an audition.~~

~~The first book of a planned series: *Still Life in Motion, Life in Motion, Still in Motion, Still In, Still Still, and In In.* Only the first book was written.~~

~~The Reading Stories section of the book, particularly *Reading Fundamentalisms* and *Referencing for Cocteau Parties* were based on lectures S{E}AN? gave to a very small group of elementary school children who liked school.~~

In *Blinkpipe* when the narrator says "I like the Gaugin…it reminds me of painting and art", the painting he is referring to is actually a Matisse. Mrs. O'Reilly doesn't correct him because it was thought that having Mrs. O'Reilly correct the narrator would make the story more languid.

The red dress in *Evocation of the Acrobat* was the same red dress used in other stories in the book. The dress was donated to S{E}AN? by Martin for the story *Minor Character*. He had hoped that Jane would wear it in the story. Martin was a minor character in the novel the story was based on but a major character in the story written about the novel. Jane tried the red dress on and liked it but in the end thought it wasn't red enough.

The paragraph at the end of *Tintoretto The Of Said* that describes Martin diving into Delores' womb was improvised.

~~The only book written in the 21st century that was not nominated for an award of any kind.~~

One Note Symphonies

~~The famous flamenco dancer Carmen Amaya posed for the photograph on the cover of the book 70 years before the book was published.~~

~~Maria, Juliet, Malene, Mylene, Sabina, Carmen, Miranda, Marrikka, Edwige, Darkbloom, and Madeline are all the same woman with different names.~~

Paya's *Don Quixote's Map of the World* was cited as an influence and inspiration for *One Note Symphonies* and for the story *diary of a composer: a one note symphony* specifically.

The story *between the last read pages of an interrupted novel* touches on *vegrandiscapillamor*, a relatively harmless psychosexual obsession.

In the story *pneumania* the relationship between music and flying is implied.

The novel that Martin is carrying in the story *between the last read pages of an interrupted novel* when he tries to deliver the Russian woman's letter is *Don Quixote's Map of the World.*

The bicycle in the story *the genealogy of the bicycle, or maria (a true story)* is the same bicycle ridden by Tamina in *The Book of Laughter and Forgetting* by Kundera.

In the story *elephant pieces*, the girl implores Martin to remember her but Martin couldn't hear her above the din of the other voices. In real life, however, Martin and the girl fell in love and got married.

The only book written in the 21st century that did not appear on any list.

The Unknowed Things

The drawing of the hand in *Theophilus God* is based on the hand of S{E}AN?.

~~Academics mistakenly compare *The History of Imagining About Blue Horses* to Borges.~~

The matador in *The Unknowed Things* is a woman dressed as a man dressed as a woman.

~~The "transition in your ear" the narrator talks about in *Beth v. Beth Singular* is a reference to a note that only Chopin could hear.~~

The book's title was originally *the world that destroyed the world* but was changed to *the unknowed things* for unknowed reasons.

~~*Chalker* is a secret word for the Swedish word for airplane.~~

In *Observations on a Future Death* Ludmilla cuts the narrator's hair too short for the scene that was supposed to follow, therefore this scene was never written in the story.

In *The World That Destroyed the World* there is ambiguity about whether Old Bobbert, Bobby, Bobbrer, Nadine, and Robert are the same person.

The first owl drawn by the boy in the *The Drawer of Owls* was found on the bathroom mirror.

~~The only book written in the 21st century that was not heralded.~~

The Dictionary of Coincidences, Volume I (Hi)

My Collection of Large Nurses was based on barely remembered events.

~~The book "Death Milks the Cow" in *The Foreword Incident* was an international best-seller of the espionage western genre.~~

~~The crime scene report in *They Say You Haven't Made It Until Your Mugshot Hits the Street* was reprinted word for word.~~

The screenplay *Screenplay from the dictionary of coincidences, volume i (hi) trailer: Unfold Freedom, Unfold* was made into a film titled "Sequence Disruptor 9". The running time was 5:21. Genesis 5:21 reads "When Enoch had lived 65 years, he became the father of Methuselah."

~~*The Tag Was Tender* includes a photograph of a pylon. The pylon was later put in the back of a truck where it stayed for months until it was used again.~~

The boy looking at the rune that was tagged with S{E}AN? is now 8 years old. He has been suspended from school 15 times in the last year for spray-painting the word "pears" on school environs.

The Dictionary of Coincidences, Volume I (Hi) is a love story.

~~The only book written in the 21st century that wasn't recommended.~~

Epilogue: Coming Soon: Superpowers for Ordinary People

'THE BRAIN THRUST!'

the BRAIN thrust!

Of all the devastating superpowers for ordinary people the BRAIN thrust is probably the second most difficult to master. I don't know if that's true but I have never been able to master the most powerful superpower for ordinary people (hint!). The BRAIN thrust looks like it's just used for defense but it can quickly change the outcome of a contest by stunning your opponent. I was practicing my superpowers for ordinary people while my friend was doing his homework. I was already finished with my homework. I was actually in the middle of practicing the QUICK cat/FIST OF STRONG combination when my friend asked me what the answer to 18 x 36 was because he ran out of room on his paper to work out the multiplication. I completely stopped my move. Or I was completely stopped in the middle of my move—somewhere in the middle of the QUICK cat—because my BRAIN was thrusted. He could have used any superpower on me while my BRAIN was thrusted because I was completely helpless.

But then we noticed something strange. Since he also didn't know the answer to the question he asked, he was stopped in middle of what he was doing (just sitting there doing his homework) because he apparently thrusted his own BRAIN by not knowing the answer to the question he asked me. So we experimented with the BRAIN thrust and figured out that if you use the BRAIN thrust you have to know the answer to the question that you're asking or you end up thrusting your own BRAIN. If your opponent knows the answer to the question you're asking then you also end up thrusting your own BRAIN. So we decided to start learning more things at school just in case. And not just in school. We decided to learn more things all the time.

"games all day"

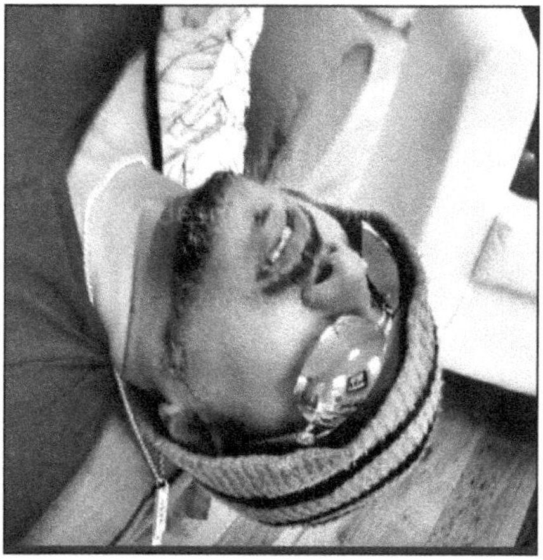

MAJus

www.ingramcontent.com/pod-product-compliance
Lightning Source LLC
Chambersburg PA
CBHW041140170626
46815CB00007B/336
* 9 7 8 0 9 8 5 2 1 3 3 6 7 *